PENGUIN CLASSICS

My Friend Maigret

'I love reading Simenon. He makes me think of Chekhov'
— William Faulkner

'A truly wonderful writer . . . marvellously readable – lucid, simple, absolutely in tune with the world he creates'
— Muriel Spark

'Few writers have ever conveyed with such a sure touch, the bleakness of human life' — A. N. Wilson

'One of the greatest writers of the twentieth century . . . Simenon was unequalled at making us look inside, though the ability was masked by his brilliance at absorbing us obsessively in his stories' — *Guardian*

'A novelist who entered his fictional world as if he were part of it' — Peter Ackroyd

'The greatest of all, the most genuine novelist we have had in literature' — André Gide

'Superb . . . The most addictive of writers . . . A unique teller of tales' — *Observer*

'The mysteries of the human personality are revealed in all their disconcerting complexity' — Anita Brookner

'A writer who, more than any other crime novelist, combined a high literary reputation with popular appeal' – P. D. James

'A supreme writer . . . Unforgettable vividness' – *Independent*

'Compelling, remorseless, brilliant' — John Gray

'Extraordinary masterpieces of the twentieth century'
— John Banville

GEORGES SIMENON

My Friend Maigret

Translated by SHAUN WHITESIDE

PENGUIN BOOKS

PENGUIN CLASSICS

UK | USA | Canada | Ireland | Australia
India | New Zealand | South Africa

Penguin Books is part of the Penguin Random House group of companies
whose addresses can be found at global.penguinrandomhouse.com.

First published in French as *Mon ami Maigret* by Presses de la Cité 1949
This translation first published 2016
002

Set in Dante MT Std 12.5/15 pt
Typeset by Palimpsest Book Production Limited, Falkirk, Stirlingshire
Printed in Great Britain by Clays Ltd, St Ives plc

ISBN: 978-0-241-20639-3

www.greenpenguin.co.uk

MIX
Paper from
responsible sources
FSC® C018179

Penguin Random House is committed to a
sustainable future for our business, our readers
and our planet. This book is made from Forest
Stewardship Council® certified paper.

Contents

1. The Very Agreeable Mr Pyke

'So you were in the doorway of your establishment?'

'Yes, inspector, sir.'

There was no point going over it all again. Four or five times Maigret had tried to persuade him to say just 'inspector'. What did it matter? What did any of it matter?

'A grey car, a big sports car, stopped for a moment, and a man got out, almost acrobatically, is that what you said?'

'Yes, inspector, sir.'

'To get into your club he had to pass right in front of you, and he even jostled you slightly. And yet, over the door there is a neon sign.'

'It's purple, inspector, sir.'

'So?'

'So nothing.'

'It's because your sign is purple that you're incapable of recognizing the individual who, a moment later, opened the velvet door and emptied his revolver into your barman?'

The man's name was Caracci or Caraccini (Maigret had to consult the file each time). He was short (he wore high heels), had the face of a Corsican (they all look a bit like Napoleon) and had an enormous yellow diamond on his finger.

It had been going on since eight o'clock in the morning

and it was now striking eleven. It had even, in fact, been going on since the middle of the night, because everyone they had picked up on Rue Fontaine, in the club where the barman had been killed, had spent the night at the station. Three or four inspectors, including Janvier and Torrence, had already dealt with Caracci, or Caraccini, without getting anything out of him.

Even though it was May, it had been raining as if it was the depths of autumn. It had been raining like that for four or five days, and the roofs, the window-sills, the umbrellas bore reflections like the water of the Seine, which the inspector saw when he lowered his head.

Mr Pyke didn't move. He stayed sitting on his chair, in a corner, as stiff as if he was in a waiting room, and it was starting to get exasperating. His eyes, slowly, moved from the inspector to the little man and from the little man to the inspector, and it was impossible to guess what was going on in the English policeman's brain.

'You know, Caracci, that your attitude could cost you dear, and that your club could easily be closed for good?'

The Corsican, unintimidated, gave Maigret an almost complicit glance, smiled and with his ringed finger smoothed the black commas of his moustache.

'I have always been law-abiding, inspector, sir. Just ask your colleague Priollet.'

Even though there had been a death, this case was in fact the concern of Inspector Priollet, head of the Drug Squad, because of the particular milieu in which it had taken place. Unfortunately Priollet was in the Jura, at the funeral of some relative or other.

'So you're refusing to speak?'

'I'm not refusing, inspector, sir.'

Maigret, heavily, gruffly, went and opened the door.

'Lucas! Give him another going-over.'

Oh! The look that Mr Pyke fixed on him! Mr Pyke might have been the nicest man on earth, but there were moments when Maigret surprised himself by hating him. Just as he did with his brother-in-law, whose name was Mouthon. Once a year, in the spring, Mouthon disembarked at the Gare de l'Est in the company of his wife, Madame Maigret's sister.

He too was the nicest man on earth; he wouldn't have hurt a fly. As for his wife, she was gaiety personified, and as soon as she arrived at the apartment on Boulevard Richard-Lenoir she grabbed an apron to help with the housework. On the first day it was perfect. On the second day, it was almost as perfect.

'We're leaving tomorrow,' Mouthon would announce.

'Oh, no! Oh, no!' Madame Maigret would reply. 'Why leave so soon?'

'We don't want to get in the way.'

'Never in a thousand years!'

Maigret too would announce with great conviction: 'Never in a thousand years!'

On the third day he would be wishing that some unexpected job would come up to stop him having dinner at home. And yet never, since his sister-in-law had married Mouthon and the couple came to see them every year, never, ever, had one of those affairs that keep you away from home for days and nights on end come up at that exact moment.

3

By the fifth day he and his wife would be exchanging desperate glances, and the Mouthons would stay for nine days, invariably pleasant, charming, considerate, as discreet as anyone could be, so that you ended up reproaching yourself even more for coming to hate them.

It was the same with Mr Pyke. However, it had only been three days since he had accompanied Maigret on all his comings and goings. Once, during the holidays, they had said carelessly to the Mouthons: 'Why don't you come and spend a week in Paris in the spring? We have a spare room that is always empty.'

They had come.

Likewise, a few weeks before, the chief of police had paid an official visit to the lord mayor of London. The mayor had shown him around the offices of the celebrated Scotland Yard, and the chief of police had been pleasantly surprised to note that the senior officers of the English police knew Maigret by reputation and were interested in his methods.

'Why not come and see him work?' the excellent fellow had asked.

They had taken him at his word. Like the Mouthons. Inspector Pyke had been sent, and for three days he had been following Maigret everywhere, as discreetly and as efficiently as it was possible to be. But he was still there.

In spite of his thirty-five or forty years, he looked so young that he might have been taken for a serious student. He was clearly intelligent, perhaps even acutely so. He looked, listened and thought. He thought so much that you could almost hear him think, and it became tiring. It was a little as if Maigret had been placed under observation. All his gestures, all his words had been picked over inside the skull of the impassive Mr Pyke.

And yet for three days there had been nothing interesting to do. Routine. Paperwork. Uninteresting interrogations, like that of Caracci.

They had reached a silent understanding, he and Pyke. For example, just as the nightclub owner had been brought into the inspectors' office, and the door carefully closed behind him, the Englishman gave him an unambiguous look:

'A beating?'

Probably, yes. You don't treat people like Caracci with kid gloves. And afterwards? It didn't matter. The case was entirely uninteresting. The barman was probably killed because he had stepped out of line, or because he was a member of a rival gang.

Periodically fellows like that settle their scores and kill each other, and basically it is good riddance.

Whether Caracci spoke or not, sooner or later someone would spill the beans, probably an informer. Do they have informers in England?

'Hello . . .! Yes . . . It's me . . . Who . . .? Lechat . . .? Don't know him . . . Where did you say he's calling from . . .? Porquerolles . . .? Pass him to me . . .'

The Englishman's eye was still fixed on him like the eye of God in the story of Cain.

'Hello . . .! I can't hear you . . . Lechat . . .? Yes . . . Good . . . Yes, I got that . . . Porquerolles . . . I got that too . . .'

With the receiver to his ear, he watched the rain

trickling down the window panes and thought that there might be some sun in Porquerolles, a little Mediterranean island off the coast of Hyères and Toulon. He had never been there but he had often been told about it. People came back from there brown as Bedouins. In fact, it was the first time he had been telephoned from an island, and he reflected that the telephone wires must run under the sea.

'Yes . . . What . . .? A little fair-haired fellow, in Luçon . . . Yes, in fact, I do remember . . .'

He had known an Inspector Lechat when, after some quite complicated administrative matters, he had been sent for a few months to Luçon, in the Vendée.

'Now you're part of the Draguignan flying squad, I see . . . And you're calling me from Porquerolles . . .'

There was crackling on the line. Every now and again girls could be heard talking to each other from one city to another.

'Hello! Paris . . . Paris . . . Hello! Paris . . . Paris . . .'

'Hello! Toulon . . . Is that you, Toulon? Hello! Toulon . . .'

Did phones work better on the other side of the Channel? Mr Pyke listened impassively and looked at him, and, to maintain his composure, Maigret fiddled with a pencil.

'Hello . . .! Do I know someone called Marcellin . . .? Which Marcellin . . .? What . . .! A fisherman . . .? Try to speak clearly, Lechat . . . I'm not getting a word . . . Someone who lives on a boat . . . Fine . . . So . . .? He claims he's a friend of mine . . .? Eh . . .? He claimed . . .? He's dead . . .? He was killed last night . . .? It has nothing to do with me, dear Lechat . . . It's not my area . . . He talked about

6

me all evening . . .? And you're telling me that's why he's dead . . .?'

He had set down his pencil and was trying to relight his pipe with his free hand.

'I'm taking a note of that, yes . . . Marcel . . . not Marcellin any more . . . As you wish . . . P for Paul . . . A for Arthur . . . C for cinema . . . yes . . . Pacaud . . . Have you sent the fingerprints . . .? A letter from me . . .? Headed paper . . .? Headed with what . . .? Brasserie des Ternes . . . It's possible . . . and what did I write on it . . .?'

If only Mr Pyke hadn't been there, stubbornly staring at him!

'I'll transcribe, yes . . . "Ginette is leaving tomorrow for the sanatorium. She sends you a hug. Best wishes . . ." And it's signed Maigret . . .? No, it isn't necessarily a forgery . . . I think I remember something . . . I'm going up to Records . . . Go down there . . .? You know very well that it isn't anything to do with me . . .'

He was about to hang up but he couldn't help asking a question, at the risk of surprising Mr Pyke.

'Is it sunny, where you are . . .? There's a mistral blowing . . .? But it's sunny . . .? Fine . . . As soon as I know anything I'll call you back . . . I promise . . .'

Mr Pyke didn't ask many questions but he had a way of looking that forced Maigret to speak.

'You know the island of Porquerolles?' he said, lighting his pipe at last. 'Apparently it's very beautiful, it's as beautiful as Capri and the Greek islands. A man was killed there last night, but it's not my area. A letter from me was found on his boat.'

'Is it really from you?'

'It's likely. The name Ginette rings a vague bell. Will you come with me?'

Mr Pyke knew his way around the offices of the Police Judiciaire, having been given the guided tour. In single file, they went up to the attic, where the files of everyone who came before the law were kept. Maigret almost suffered from an inferiority complex, and he was ashamed of the aged employee in long grey overalls who was sucking on Parma violets.

'Tell me, Langlois . . . By the way, is your wife better?'

'It wasn't my wife, Monsieur Maigret, it was my mother-in-law.'

'Ah! Of course. Forgive me . . . Has she had the operation?'

'She came home yesterday.'

'Could you see if you have anything in the name of Marcel Pacaud? With a *d* at the end.'

Were things better in London? They could hear the rain drumming on the roof and rushing into the gutters.

'Marcel?' the clerk asked, perched on a ladder.

'That's the one. Pass me his file.'

Apart from the fingerprints, it contained a full-face photograph and one in profile, without a collar, without a tie, in the harsh light of the Criminal Records office.

'Pacaud, Marcel-Joseph-Étienne, born in Le Havre, sailor.'

Maigret, frowning and staring at the photographs, tried to remember. The man had been thirty-five when the photographs were taken. He was thin and unhealthy-looking. A bruise above his right eye seemed to suggest that he had been seriously interrogated before being handed over to the photographer.

It was followed by quite a long list of sentences. In Le Havre, at the age of seventeen, aggravated assault. In Bordeaux a year later, more aggravated assault, along with drunkenness in a public place. Resisting arrest. Aggravated assault again in a place of ill repute in Marseille.

Maigret held the file in such a way as to let his English colleague read at the same time as him, and Mr Pyke showed no surprise, seeming to say, 'We have this on the other side of the water as well.'

'Procuring . . .'

Did they have that too? It meant that Marcel Pacaud had worked as a pimp. And as a result, he had been sent to do his military service with the Battalions of Light Infantry of Africa.

'Aggravated assault, in Nantes . . .'

'Aggravated assault, in Toulon . . .'

'A brawler,' Maigret said simply to Mr Pyke.

Then things became serious.

'Paris. Client theft.'

'What's that?'

How to explain such a thing to someone from what's probably the most prudish nation on earth!

'It's a kind of theft, but it's a theft committed in particular circumstances. When a gentleman goes with a lady he doesn't know to a more or less seedy hotel and then complains that his wallet is missing, that's called client theft. The lady almost always has an accomplice, you understand?'

'I understand.'

There were three accusations of this type of theft in Marcel Pacaud's file, and each one mentioned a certain Ginette.

Then things became still more serious, with a knife attack that Pacaud was supposed to have made on a recalcitrant client.

'I think we might be talking about bad guys here?' suggested Mr Pyke, whose French was terribly nuanced, so nuanced that it was capable of irony.

'Exactly. I wrote to him, I remember. I don't know how such things are done in your country.'

'Very correctly.'

'I don't doubt it. Here we sometimes knock them about. We're not always nice to them. But the funny thing is that they rarely resent us for it. They know we're doing our job. From interrogation to interrogation, we end up knowing each other.'

'Is he the one who said you were his friend?'

'I'm sure he meant it. I particularly remember his daughter, and what reminds me of her the most is the headed paper. If we have a chance I'll show you the Brasserie des Ternes. It's very comfortable, and the sauerkraut is excellent. Do you like sauerkraut?'

'Now and then,' the Englishman replied unenthusiastically.

'In the afternoon and evening there are always some

ladies sitting by a pedestal table, and that's where Ginette worked. She was a Breton, from a village near St Malo. She had started as a maid working for a local butcher. She adored Pacaud, and he was moved to tears when he talked about her. Does that surprise you?'

Nothing surprised Mr Pyke, whose face showed no emotion.

'I took a bit of a passing interest in them. She was riddled with tuberculosis. She had never wanted to have treatment because it would have taken her away from her Marcel. When he was in jail, I persuaded her to go and see one of my friends, a lung specialist, and he had her admitted to a sanatorium in Savoie. That's all.'

'Is that what you wrote to Pacaud?'

'Yes, exactly. Pacaud was in Fresnes, and I didn't have time to go there.'

Maigret handed the file back to Langlois and set off down the stairs.

'Shall we have a spot of lunch?'

It was yet another problem, almost a moral dilemma. If he took Mr Pyke for lunch in too fancy a restaurant, he risked giving his colleagues from the other side of the Channel the impression that the French police spends most of its time having blow-outs. If, on the other hand, he took him to a cheap café, he might be accused of stinginess.

The same went for aperitifs. To have them? Not to have them?

'Do you think you'll go to Porquerolles?'

Did Mr Pyke fancy a trip to the South of France?

'That's not up to me. Theoretically I have no business outside of Paris and the département of the Seine.'

The sky was grey, a miserable, hopeless grey, and even the word mistral assumed a tempting sound.

'Do you like tripe?'

He took him to Les Halles for tripes à la mode de Caen and crêpes Suzette served on pretty brass plate-warmers.

'This is what we call a slack day.'

'So do we.'

What must the man from Scotland Yard think of him? He had come to study the 'Maigret methods', and Maigret had no method. All he found was a fat, rather clumsy man, who must have seemed to him like the prototype of a French civil servant. For how long was he going to follow him about like that?

At two o'clock they were back at Quai des Orfèvres, and Caracci was still there, in the glass cage-like room that served as a waiting room. It meant that they hadn't got anything out of him, and they were going to question him again.

'Has he eaten?' asked Mr Pyke.

'I don't know. Maybe. Sometimes they take them up a sandwich.'

'And the other times?'

'They let them starve for a while to help them remember.'

'The chief wants you, detective chief inspector.'

'Will you excuse me, Mr Pyke?'

That was something at least. The other man wouldn't follow him into the chief's office.

'Come in, Maigret. I've just had a phone call from Draguignan.'

'I know what it's about.'

'Lechat has contacted you, I see. Do you have a lot of work at the moment?'

'Not too much. Apart from my guest . . .'

'Is he getting on your nerves?'

'He's the most strait-laced man on earth.'

'Do you remember a man called Pacaud?'

'I remembered him when I consulted his file.'

'Don't you think it's an odd story?'

'I only know what Lechat told me on the phone, and he was trying so hard to explain that I didn't catch most of it.'

'The chief superintendent talked to me about it for a long time. He insists that you take a trip down there. In his opinion it's because of you that Pacaud was killed.'

'Because of me?'

'He can't see any other explanation for the murder. For several years Pacaud, better known under the name of Marcellin, lived in Porquerolles, on his boat. He became a popular figure. As far as I've been able to tell, he was more like a tramp than a fisherman. In the winter he lived without doing anything. In the summer he took tourists fishing around the island. No one stood to benefit from his death. He had no known enemies. He hadn't had any disputes with anyone. Nothing was stolen from him, for the excellent reason that there was nothing to be stolen.'

'How was he killed?'

'That's exactly what the chief superintendent is intrigued by.'

The chief consulted some notes that he had taken in the course of his telephone conversation.

'Since I don't know the place, it's hard for me to have an exact idea. The evening before last . . .'

'I thought I'd understood that it was yesterday . . .'

'No, the day before. A number of people had met at the Arche de Noé. It must be an inn or a café. At that time of year it seems you only see locals. Everyone knows everyone else. Marcellin was there. In the course of a more or less general conversation he mentioned you.'

'Why?'

'No idea. People like to talk about celebrities. Marcellin claimed you were his friend. Perhaps some people had cast doubts on your professional abilities? Still, he defended you with unusual passion.'

'Was he drunk?'

'He was always more or less drunk. There was a strong mistral blowing. I don't know what the mistral had to do with anything, but from what I've understood it has a certain importance. In particular it's because of the mistral that Marcellin, rather than going to sleep on his boat as he usually does, headed for a shack that stands near the harbour, where the fishermen store their nets. When they found him the next morning, he had had several bullets to the head, fired at point blank range, and one in his shoulder. The murderer emptied the whole barrel into him. Not content with that, he hit him in the face with a heavy object. It seems to have been an extremely ferocious assault.'

Maigret looked at the Seine, outside, through the curtain of rain and thought of the Mediterranean sun.

'Boisvert, the chief superintendent, is a good man. I used to know him. He isn't in the habit of getting carried away. He's just arrived in the town, but he has to leave this evening. Like Lechat he thinks that it's the conversation about you that sparked the tragedy. He's not far off claiming that it was you, somehow, who was the real target, through Marcellin. Do you understand? A man angry enough with you to attack someone who claims to be your friend and is defending you.'

'Are there such people in Porquerolles?'

'That's where Boisvert draws a blank. On an island everyone knows everybody. No one can disembark and leave again without everyone knowing. So far there isn't a single suspect. Or else we would have to suspect people counter to all appearances. What do you think?'

'I think that Mr Pyke wants to go on a trip to the South of France.'

'And what about you?'

'I think I'd like to do the same, if I could go on my own.'

'When do you leave?'

'I'll take the night train.'

'With Mr Pyke?'

'With Mr Pyke!'

Did the Englishman imagine that the French police had powerful cars to take them to crime scenes?

He must have thought, in any case, that the inspectors of the Police Judiciaire had unlimited travelling funds. Had

Maigret been right? Alone, he would have settled for a couchette. At the Gare de Lyon, he hesitated. Then, at the last minute, he took two berths in a sleeping compartment.

It was magnificent. In the corridor they met very wealthy travellers with impressive luggage. An elegant crowd, laden with flowers, was accompanying a film star to the train.

'It's the Blue Train,' Maigret murmured, as if by way of apology.

If only he had been able to know what his colleague wanted! On top of everything, they were obliged to get undressed in front of each other, and the next morning they would have to share the tiny bathroom.

'In short,' said Mr Pyke, in pyjamas and dressing gown, 'this is the start of an inquiry.'

What did he actually mean? There was something so precise about his French that you were always looking for a secret meaning in his words.

'It's an inquiry, yes.'

'Did you make a copy of Marcellin's file?'

'No. I must confess it didn't occur to me.'

'Were you worried about what became of the woman? Ginette, I think?'

'No.'

Was that a look of reproach that Mr Pyke was darting at him?

'Do you have a blank arrest warrant?'

'I don't have that either. Just a letter of request, which means I can call people in and question them.'

'Do you know Porquerolles?'

'I've never set foot there. I don't really know the South. I was on a case once in Antibes and Cannes, and what I remember most is oppressive heat and an unshakeable desire to sleep.'

'You don't like the Mediterranean?'

'Basically I don't like places where I lose the taste for work.'

'Because you like working, don't you?'

'I don't know.'

It was true. On the one hand he cursed every time a case interrupted his daily routine. On the other, as soon as he was left in peace for a few days he became sulky and almost anxious.

'Do you sleep well on trains?'

'I sleep well anywhere.'

'Doesn't the train help you think?'

'I think so little, you know!'

He was embarrassed to see the compartment full of his pipe smoke, all the more so because the Englishman didn't smoke.

'In short, you don't know the best way to approach it?'

'Quite. I don't even know if there is a way.'

'Thank you.'

It was clear that Mr Pyke had registered every one of Maigret's words and filed them neatly in his brain to use them later. It was extremely embarrassing. You could imagine him back in Scotland Yard, gathering his colleagues together (perhaps in front of a blackboard?) and announcing in his precise voice:

'An inquiry by Detective Chief Inspector Maigret . . .'

And what if it turned out to be a flop? If it was one of those cases you flounder in and only find out the solution ten years later, by pure chance? What if it was a dull case, if Lechat came running to the door the following day, announcing:

'It's finished! We've arrested the drunk who did it. He's confessed!'

What if . . . Madame Maigret hadn't put a dressing gown in his suitcase. She hadn't wanted him to take the old one, which looked like a monk's robe, and for two months he'd been meaning to buy a new one. He felt indecent in his nightshirt.

'A nightcap?' Mr Pyke suggested, holding out a silver hip flask and a beaker. 'That's what we call the last whisky before bedtime.'

He drank down a beaker of whisky. He didn't like it. Perhaps Mr Pyke didn't like the calvados that Maigret had been making him swallow for the past three days either?

He went to sleep and was aware that he was snoring. When he woke up, he saw olive trees on the banks of the Rhône and knew that they had passed Avignon.

It was sunny, and there was a light, golden mist above the river. The Englishman, clean-shaven and correct from head to toe, was standing in the corridor, his face pressed to the window. The bathroom was as clean as if it had never been used, and a discreet scent of lavender hung in the air.

Unsure yet whether he was in a good or a bad mood, Maigret grumbled as he looked in his suitcase for his razor.

'Now, it's important not to act the idiot!'

Perhaps it was Mr Pyke's impeccable correctness that made him seem unrefined . . .

2. The Customers at the Arche

Overall, the first round had gone rather well. Which isn't to say that there was competition between the two men, at least not in professional terms. If Mr Pyke was more or less involved in Maigret's police work, it was only as an onlooker.

Maigret, however, was thinking 'first round', while being aware that it was not the right phrase. Does one not have the right, in one's head, to use one's own language?

When he had joined the English inspector in the corridor of the Pullman, for example, it was clear that Mr Pyke, taken by surprise, had not had time to erase the look of wonder that transfigured him. Was it simply reserve, because a Scotland Yard officer should not concern himself with the sunrise over one of the most beautiful landscapes in the world? Or was the Englishman loath to display an admiration that he considered indecent in front of a foreign witness?

Maigret had no hesitation in silently scoring himself a point.

To be fair, in the restaurant car, Mr Pyke had marked one up in turn. A trivial matter. A faint pinch of the nostrils at the arrival of the bacon and eggs, incontestably inferior to those of his own country.

'You don't know the Mediterranean, Mr Pyke?'

'I usually spend my holidays in Sussex. But I did once travel to Egypt. The sea was grey and stormy, and it rained throughout the whole crossing.'

And Maigret, who, deep down, was not too fond of the Midi, felt tickled by a desire to defend it.

One off note: the maitre d', who had recognized the inspector, having presumably served him elsewhere in the past, came over immediately after his breakfast and asked him in an ingratiating voice:

'Can I serve you a little something to drink, as usual?'

And yet the previous day, or the day before that, the inspector had noticed, as if butter wouldn't melt in his mouth, that an English gentleman never touches strong drink before late afternoon.

The arrival in Hyères was, without a shadow of a doubt, a round in Maigret's favour. The palm trees around the railway station were motionless, fixed in a Saharan sun. It looked as if there was a big market on that morning, a fair or a fête, because the carts, vans and heavy trucks were moving pyramids of fruits, vegetables and flowers.

Mr Pyke, like Maigret, was a little out of breath. It really felt as if they were stepping into another world, and they were embarrassed to be entering it in the dark clothes that had been suited to the rainy streets of Paris the evening before.

They should, like Inspector Lechat, have been wearing a pale-blue suit with an open-necked shirt, and with a raw splash of sunburn on their foreheads. Maigret hadn't recognized him straight away, because he remembered his name better than his appearance. Lechat, who was dodging in and out among the porters, almost looked like a little boy, small and thin, hatless, and with espadrilles on his feet.

'This way, chief!'

Was that a point to him? Because if this Mr Pyke fellow registered everything, there was no way of telling what he put in the good column and what he wrote in the bad. Formally, Lechat should have called Maigret 'sir', because he was not part of his service. But there were few policemen in France who could resist the pleasure of calling him 'chief' with affectionate familiarity.

'Mr Pyke, you already know of Inspector Lechat. Lechat, allow me to introduce Mr Pyke of Scotland Yard.'

'Are they on the case as well?'

Lechat was so immersed in the Marcellin story that he wasn't even slightly surprised that it might have become an international affair.

'Mr Pyke is here to study our methods.'

As they passed through the crowd, Maigret wondered why Lechat was walking so oddly, constantly darting sideways and craning his neck.

'Let's get a move on,' he said. 'My car is by the gate.'

It was a little police car. Only once they were in did the inspector sigh:

'I think you should be careful. Everyone thinks you're the one they're after.'

So, in the crowd, a few moments before, it had been Maigret that tiny Lechat had been trying to protect!

'Shall I take you straight to the island? Anything you need to do in Hyères?'

And they drove. The land was flat and deserted, the road lined with tamarinds and the occasional palm tree, then white salt flats on the right. Their sense of being in a strange country was as total as if they had been transported to Africa, with a china-blue sky, a perfectly still atmosphere.

'The mistral?' Maigret asked with a hint of irony.

'It stopped all of a sudden last night. Not before time. It blew for nine days, and that's enough to put everyone on edge.'

Maigret was sceptical. People in the North – and the North begins somewhere around Lyon – have never taken the mistral seriously. So Mr Pyke also had an excuse for being indifferent.

'No one has left the island. You'll be able to question everyone who was there when Marcellin was murdered. The fishermen weren't at sea that night, because of the storm. But a torpedo-boat from Toulon and several submarines were carrying out manoeuvres off the coast of the island. I've called the Admiralty. They are categorical. No boat made the crossing.'

'Which means that the murderer is still on the island.'

'You'll see.'

Lechat was playing the old hand who knows the places and the people. Maigret was the newcomer, which is always a disagreeable part to play. The car, half an hour later, stopped on a rocky headland where all that could be seen was an inn in the Provençal style and some fishermen's cottages painted pink and pale blue.

A point to France, because it was breathtaking. The sea was an incredible blue, the kind that one normally sees only on postcards, and down on the horizon an island stretched out languidly in the middle of the iridescent surface, with very green hills and red and yellow rocks.

At the end of the wooden jetty, a fishing boat waited, painted pale green with a white gunwale.

'It's for us. I asked Gabriel to bring it to me and wait for you. The boat that does the regular service, the *Cormoran*, only comes at eight in the morning and five in the afternoon. Gabriel is a Galli. I'll explain. There are Gallis and Morins. Almost everyone on the island belongs to one of those two families.'

Lechat carried the suitcases, which looked bigger in his hands. The engine was already running. It was all a little unreal, and it was hard to think that they were only here to deal with a dead man.

'I didn't offer to show you the body. It's in Hyères. The autopsy took place yesterday morning.'

It was about three miles between the headland of Giens and Porquerolles. As they advanced across the silken water, the outline of the island grew clearer, with its capes and bays, its old forts among the greenery and right in the middle the white bell-tower of a church straight out of a construction set.

'Do you think I could find myself a swimming-costume?' the Englishman asked Lechat.

Maigret hadn't thought of that and, leaning over the handrail, he suddenly felt a hint of vertigo as he saw the bottom of the sea sliding along beneath the boat. The water must have been ten metres deep, but it was so clear that you could make out the tiniest details of the undersea landscape. And it was a real landscape, with its plains covered with greenery, its rocky hills, its gorges and precipices, among which the shoals of fish passed like herds of sheep.

Slightly embarrassed, as if he had been caught playing a childish game, Maigret looked at Mr Pyke, but only to score one more point: the inspector from Scotland Yard, almost as moved as he was himself, was also staring at the bottom of the water.

It's only later on that you work out the layout of places. At first sight everything looks strange. The port was tiny, with a jetty on the left, a rocky headland, covered with maritime pines, on the right. In the background, red roofs, white and pink houses among the palm trees, mimosas and tamarinds.

Had Maigret ever seen mimosas except in the baskets of the little flower-sellers of Paris? He couldn't remember whether mimosas had been in bloom when he had been on the case in Antibes and Cannes some years earlier.

A handful of people were waiting on the jetty. There were also some fishermen in boats painted like Christmas decorations.

They watched them disembark. Were the people on land forming different groups? Maigret would only look into the details later. For example, a man in white, with a white cap on his head, greeted him by bringing his hand to his temple, and he didn't recognize him straight away.

'It's Charlot!' Lechat whispered in his ear.

The name didn't mean anything to him at first. A kind of barefoot colossus, who didn't utter a word, loaded the luggage on to a wheelbarrow and pushed it towards the village square.

Maigret, Pyke and Lechat followed. And, behind them, the locals followed too; all in a strange silence.

The square was vast and bare, framed with eucalyptus trees and colourfully painted houses with, at the top, the little yellow church with the white bell-tower. They saw several cafés with shady terraces.

'I could have booked you some rooms at the Grand Hôtel. It's been open for a fortnight.'

It was quite a large building which overlooked the port, and a man in a chef's uniform was standing in the doorway.

'I thought it better to put you up at the Arche de Noé. I'll explain why.'

There had already been lots of things that the inspector had to explain. The terrace of the Arche, on the square, was wider than the others, bounded by a low wall and by green plants. Inside it was cool, a little dark, which was not at all unpleasant, and one was immediately struck by the sharp smell of cooking and white wine.

Another man dressed as a chef, but without a hat. He came forwards with his hand outstretched and a radiant smile on his face.

'Delighted to welcome you, Monsieur Maigret. I've given you the best room. You'll have a little local white wine?'

Lechat whispered:

'That's Paul, the landlord.'

There were red tiles on the floor. The bar was a real bistro counter, made of tin. The white wine was cool, quite young, full-flavoured.

'Your health, Monsieur Maigret. I didn't dare to hope that I would one day have the honour of receiving you here.'

It didn't occur to him that he owed the visit to a crime. No one seemed concerned with Marcellin's death. The groups they had seen a moment before by the jetty were now in the square and were moving imperceptibly towards the Arche de Noé. Some people were even sitting down on the terrace.

In short, what mattered was the arrival of Maigret in flesh and blood, exactly as if he had been a film star.

Did he cut a fine figure? Did the people of Scotland Yard have more self-assurance at the start of an investigation? Mr Pyke looked at everything and said nothing.

'I would like to freshen up a little,' Maigret sighed at last, after drinking two glasses of white wine.

'Jojo! Will you show Monsieur Maigret to his room? Will your friend come up as well, inspector?'

Jojo was a little dark maid, dressed in black, with a big smile and little pointed breasts.

The whole building smelled of bouillabaisse and saffron. At the top of the stairs, red-tiled like the café, there were only three or four rooms; they had reserved the finest one for the inspector, with one window looking out on the square and the other out on the sea. Should he offer it to Mr Pyke? It was too late. He had already been shown to a different door.

'Do you need anything, Monsieur Maigret? The bath-room is at the end of the corridor. I think there is some hot water.'

Lechat had followed him. It was natural. It was normal. And yet he didn't invite him in. He felt it would be a kind of rudeness towards his English colleague. Mr Pyke might have imagined that something was being hidden from him, that he wasn't being allowed to witness the whole of the investigation.

'I'll be down in a few minutes, Lechat.'

He would have liked to find a pleasant word for the police officer, who had been looking after him so solicitously. He thought he remembered that in Luçon there had been much mention of his wife. Standing in the doorway, he asked him, in a cordial and familiar voice:

'And how is the excellent Madame Lechat?'

And the poor fellow stammered:

'Didn't you know? She left. She left me eight years ago.'

What a blunder! It came back to him all of a sudden. When they talked about Madame Lechat, in Luçon, it was because she was frantically deceiving her husband.

In his room he did nothing but take off his jacket, wash his hands and face and brush his teeth, and stretch by the window, before lying down on the bed as if to test the springs. The decoration was old-fashioned and genteel, still with that fine smell of southern cooking that filled all the corners of the house. Because it was hot, he thought of going downstairs in shirt-sleeves but thought that would make him look like a holiday-maker and put his jacket on instead.

When he reached the ground floor, several people were at the bar, mostly men in fishermen's clothes. Lechat was waiting for him on the threshold.

'Would you like to take a walk, chief?'

'It would be preferable for us to wait for Mr Pyke.'

'He's already outside.'

'Where?'

'In the water. Paul lent him a swimming-costume.'

They walked mechanically towards the port. The slope of the ground led them there all by itself. They felt that everyone must be bound to follow the same path.

'I think, chief, that you've got to be very cautious. The man who killed Marcellin is angry with you, and he will try to get you.'

'We should wait until Mr Pyke has come out of the water.'

Lechat pointed to a head that emerged from the water beyond the boats.

'Is he part of the investigation?'

'He's observing. We mustn't look as if we're plotting behind his back.'

'We would have had more peace at the Grand Hôtel. It closes during the winter. It's only just opened, and there's no one there. Except everyone meets up at Paul's place. That's where the whole thing started, that's where Marcellin talked about you, claiming that you were his friend.'

'Let's wait for Mr Pyke.'

'Do you want to question people in front of him?'

'I'll have to.'

Lechat pulled a face but didn't dare to protest.

'Where are you going to summon them? The town hall is just about the only place. One room, with benches, a table, the 14th of July flags and a bust of Marianne. The mayor runs the grocer's shop beside the Arche de Noé. That's him over there, pushing a handcart.'

Mr Pyke got to his feet beside a boat attached to its chain and strolled through the water, splashing in the sunlight.

'The water is marvellous,' he said.

'If you like, we could wait here while you go and get dressed.'

'I'm very comfortable.'

This time he scored a point of his own. He was, in fact, just as much at ease in his swimming-costume, with drops of salt water trickling along his thin body, as in his grey suit.

He pointed to a black yacht, not in the port, but at anchor a few cables' lengths away. It was flying the British flag.

'Who's that?'

Lechat explained:

'The boat is called *North Star*. It comes here almost every year. It belongs to Mrs Ellen Wilcox: it's also, I believe, the name of a kind of whisky. She's the owner of the Wilcox whisky company.'

'Is she young?'

'She's quite well preserved. She lives on board with her secretary, Philippe de Moricourt, and two crewmen. There is another Englishman on the island, who lives there all year. You can see his house from here. It's the one flanked by a minaret.'

Mr Pyke looked far from enchanted at the idea of meeting his compatriots.

'He's Major Bellam, but people on the island call him simply "major", and sometimes Teddy.'

'I suppose he's a major in the Indian army?'

'I don't know.'

'Does he drink a lot?'

'A lot. You'll see him this evening at the Arche. You'll see everyone at the Arche, including Mrs Wilcox and her secretary.'

'Were they there when Marcellin spoke?' Maigret asked for the sake of saying something, because really he wasn't yet interested in anything.

'They were. Everyone, practically, was at the Arche, like every evening. In a week or two, the tourists will start pouring in, and life will be different. For now it's no longer quite winter, when the inhabitants are alone on the island, and it isn't yet what we call the season. Only the regulars have arrived. I don't know if you understand. Most of them have been coming here for years and know everyone. The major has been living at the Minaret for eight years. The villa next door belongs to Monsieur Émile.'

Lechat looked at Maigret with apparent hesitation. Perhaps in front of the Englishman he too was feeling a kind of patriotic modesty.

'Monsieur Émile?'

'You know him. Or at any rate he knows you. He lives with his mother, old Justine, who is one of the most famous women on the Côte d'Azur. She owns Fleurs, in Marseille, Sirènes in Nice, two or three houses in Toulon, in Béziers, in Avignon . . .'

Had Mr Pyke worked out what kind of houses he was talking about?

'Justine is seventy-nine. I thought she was older, because Monsieur Émile claims to be sixty-five. Apparently she had him when she was fourteen. She told me that yesterday. They're very quiet, both of them, they don't keep company. Hang on, that's Monsieur Émile that you can see in his garden, in a white suit with a pith helmet. He looks like a white mouse. He has a little boat, like everyone, but he barely goes further than the end of the jetty, where he just spends hours fishing for wrasse.'

'What are those?' asked Mr Pyke, whose skin was starting to dry.

'Wrasse? A pretty little fish, with red and black on its back. It's not bad fried, but it's not serious fishing. Do you understand?'

'I understand.'

All three of them walked along the sand, passing the backs of the houses whose façades looked on to the square.

'There's another character from the underworld. We'll probably be eating at the table next to him. He's Charlot. Just now, when we got off the boat, he said hello to you, chief. I asked him to stay, and he didn't protest. It's even curious that no one asked to leave. They're all very calm, very well behaved.'

'The big yacht?'

There was indeed a huge white yacht, not very pretty, completely made of metal, which almost filled the port.

'The *Alcyon*? It's there all year round. It belongs to an industrialist from Lyon, Monsieur Jaureguy, who doesn't use it more than a week a year. He takes it out to go swimming, all by himself, just within earshot of the island.

There are two sailors on board, two Bretons, who lead a good life.'

Did the Englishman expect to see Maigret taking notes? He saw him smoking his pipe and looking lazily around as he listened distractedly to Lechat.

'Look at the little green boat beside it, which is a funny shape. The cabin is tiny, and yet there are two people, a man and a woman, living on it. They have used the sail to rig up a tent over the deck, and most of the time that's where they sleep. That's where they do their cooking and washing. They aren't regulars on the island. They were found one morning moored to the place where they are now. The man's name is Jef de Greef and he's Dutch. He's a painter. He's only twenty-four. The girl is called Anna, and she isn't his wife. I've got their papers. She's eighteen. She was born in Ostend. She's always half naked and sometimes more than half. As soon as evening falls you can see them both swimming at the end of the jetty without any clothes on at all.'

Lechat was careful to add for the benefit of Mr Pyke:

'It's true that Mrs Wilcox, if the fishermen are to be believed, does the same around her yacht.'

They were being watched, from a distance. Still little groups that looked as if they had nothing else to do all day.

'Another fifty metres and you'll see Marcellin's boat.'

The port was now lined not with the backs of the houses on the square, but by villas, most of them buried away in greenery.

'They're all empty, apart from two,' Lechat explained. 'I'll tell you who they belong to. This one belongs to

Monsieur Émile and his mother. I've already spoken to you about the Minaret. '

A retaining wall separated the gardens from the sea. Each villa had its own little jetty. A typical boat of the region, pointed at both ends and about six metres long, was moored to one of the jetties.

'That's Marcellin's boat.'

It was dirty, and the deck was untidy. Against the wall there was a kind of fireplace made of big stones, a big pot, churns blackened by smoke, empty litre bottles.

'Is it true that you knew him, chief? In Paris?'

'In Paris, yes.'

'What people around here refuse to believe is that he was born in Le Havre. Everyone is sure that he was a real southerner. He had the accent. He was an odd fish. He lived on his boat. Every now and again he took a trip to the continent, as he called it, that is, he went and moored on the jetty in Giens, St Tropez or Lavandou. When the weather was too bad, he went to sleep in the shack that you can see a bit above the port. That's where the fishermen boil their nets. He didn't need anything. The butcher gave him a piece of meat every now and again. He didn't fish much, and then only in the summer, when he took tourists out. There are a few like him along the coast.'

'Do you have them in England as well?' Maigret asked Mr Pyke.

'It's too cold. We only have the dock rats, in the ports.'

'Did he drink?'

'White wine. When we needed him to give us a hand with something, we paid him with a bottle of white wine.

He also won drinks at boules, because he was very good at boules. I found the letter on the boat. I'll give it to you shortly. I left it at the town hall.'

'No other papers?'

'His army pass book, a photograph of a woman and that's all. Odd that he kept your letter, don't you think?'

Maigret didn't find it particularly surprising. He would have liked to talk about it to Mr Pyke, whose trunks were drying in patches. That would be for later.

'Do you want to visit the shack? I locked it. I've got the key in my pocket: I'll have to give it back to the fishermen, who need it.'

No shack right now. Maigret was hungry. And he was also in a hurry to see his English colleague in less skimpy clothing. It embarrassed him, for no precise reason. He wasn't in the habit of leading an investigation in the company of a man in a swimming-costume.

He needed to drink a bit more white wine. It was clearly a tradition on the island. Mr Pyke went upstairs to get dressed and came down again tieless and with his shirt collar open, like Lechat, and he had had time to buy himself, probably at the mayor's grocer's shop, a pair of blue canvas espadrilles.

The fishermen, who probably wanted to speak to them, didn't dare to as yet. The Arche had two rooms: the café, where the bar was, and a smaller room with tables covered with red checked tablecloths. Their places had been set. Two tables away, Charlot was busy tasting sea urchins.

This time, once again, he brought his hand to his temple, looking at Maigret. Then he added, indifferently:

'All right?'

They had spent some hours, perhaps a whole night, alone together in Maigret's office, five or six years before. The inspector had forgotten his real name. Everyone knew him by the name of Charlot.

He did a little of everything, 'recruiting' for the brothels of the Midi, smuggling cocaine and some other products; he also worked on the horse-races and, at election time, became one of the most active electoral agents on the coast.

He was very meticulous about his appearance; he had measured gestures, an imperturbable composure and a little spark of irony in his eyes.

'Do you like Mediterranean cuisine, Mr Pyke?'

'I don't know it.'

'Would you like to try it?'

'I'd be delighted.'

And Paul, the landlord, suggested:

'Some little birds, to start? I have some skewers that I was brought this morning.'

They were robins, Paul was unfortunate enough to announce, serving the Englishman, who could not help looking with great emotion at his plate.

'You see, inspector, that I've taken some trouble.'

Charlot, from his table, still eating, spoke to them in an undertone.

'I've been waiting for you patiently. I didn't even ask your colleague for permission to leave.'

Quite a long silence.

'I'm at your disposal, whenever you like. Paul will tell you that I didn't leave the Arche that evening.'

'Are you in a hurry?'

'To do what?'

'Prove your innocence?'

'I'm preparing the ground, that's all. I'm doing my best to ensure that you don't get too lost. Because you're going to get lost. I get lost and I'm from here.'

'Did you know Marcellin?'

'I've drunk with him a hundred times, if that's what you mean. Is it true that you've brought someone from Scotland Yard with you?' He cynically examined Mr Pyke as a curious object. 'It's none of his business. It's none of your business either, if you'll allow me to give you my opinion. You know I've always been up front. We've already made things quite clear to each other. Neither of us got angry. What's the name of that fat little sergeant who was in your office? Lucas! How is Lucas? Paul! Jojo . . .! Hey . . .!'

As no one answered him he headed towards the kitchen and came back a little later with a plate that smelled of aioli.

'Am I keeping you from your conversation?'

'Not at all.'

'In that case, all you'd have to do was politely ask me to shut up. I'm thirty-four years old. To be precise, I turned thirty-four yesterday, which means that I'm starting to find my way around. I've had some conversations with your colleagues, in Paris, Marseille and elsewhere. They didn't always treat me very nicely. We didn't always understand each other, but there is something that everyone will tell you: Charlot never got his hands dirty.'

It was true, if it meant that he had never killed anyone.

He must have had a good dozen sentences on his record, but for relatively minor crimes.

'Do you know why I come here regularly? I like the place, obviously, and Paul's a friend. But there's another reason. Look in the left-hand corner. The slot machine. It's mine, and I have about fifty of them from Marseille to St Raphael. It's not exactly above board. Sometimes these gentlemen get nasty and take one or two off me.'

Poor Mr Pyke, who had been anxious to eat up his little birds, in spite of his delicate feelings! Now he was sniffing the aioli, struggling to conceal his fear.

'You're wondering why I'm talking so much, aren't you?'

'I haven't been wondering anything at all.'

'It's not my custom. I'll tell you anyway. Here, on the island, I mean, there are two guys who will end up taking the blame for this whole business: Émile and me. We both know the score. People are nice to us, particularly if we pay our way. People exchange glances. They say under their breath, "They're up to no good" or "Look at him. He's a hard man!" But still, as soon as there's a setback, we get it in the neck.

'I've understood, and that's why I've stayed out of trouble. I have friends waiting for me along the coast and I haven't even tried to call them. Your sweet little inspector, has his eye on me, and for two days he's been dying to lock me up. Well, I'll tell you plainly, and to help you avoid making a mistake: it wouldn't be fair.

'That's all. After that, at your service.'

Maigret waited for Charlot to leave, with a toothpick

between his lips, before quietly asking his colleague from Scotland Yard:

'Do you sometimes make friends among your clients in England?'

'Not quite like that.'

'Meaning?'

'We don't have a lot of people like that gentleman. Some things don't happen in the same way. Do you understand?'

Why did Maigret think about Mrs Wilcox and her young secretary? Some things, indeed, didn't happen in the same way.

'For example, for a long time I've had a relationship, cordial enough, let's say, with a famous jewel thief. We have a lot of jewel thieves. It's something of a national speciality. They're almost always cultivated people who come from the best colleges and frequent smart clubs. We have the same difficulty as you do with people like this gentleman, or the one he called Monsieur Émile: to catch them red-handed. For four years I had been trailing the thief I mentioned. He knew. We often found ourselves drinking whisky together in a bar. We also had a number of chess games together.'

'And did you catch him?'

'Never. In the end we reached what we call a "gentle-men's agreement". Do you understand the term? I kept getting in his way, so much so that last year he didn't even attempt anything and ended up in abject poverty. For my part, I wasted a lot of time over him. I advised him to go and exercise his talents elsewhere. Is that what you're talking about?'

'Did he go and steal jewels in New York?'

'I think he's in Paris,' Mr Pyke calmly corrected him, picking up a toothpick of his own.

A second bottle of island wine, which Jojo had brought without being asked, was more than half empty. The landlord came and suggested:

'A little glass of marc? After the aioli it's compulsory.'

It was lukewarm, almost cool in the room, while dense sunlight, noisy with flies, weighed down on the square.

Charlot, probably to aid his digestion, had just started a game of boules with a fisherman, and half a dozen others were following the game.

'Will you do the interrogations at the town hall?' asked little Lechat, who didn't seem to be in any way lethargic.

Maigret nearly replied, 'What interrogations?'

But they couldn't forget Mr Pyke, who was gulping down his marc and seemed almost to be enjoying it.

'At the town hall, yes . . .'

He would rather have gone for a siesta.

3. Benoît's Coffin

Monsieur Félicien Jamet, the mayor (known, of course, simply as Félicien), came with his key to open the door of the town hall for them. Twice already, while watching him cross the square, Maigret had wondered what it was that was strange about his bearing and suddenly understood: perhaps because he also sold lamps, paraffin, galvanized iron wire and nails, Félicien, rather than wearing the yellowish apron of grocers, had adopted the grey overall of the ironmonger. He wore it very long, almost down to his ankles. Did he have trousers on underneath? Did he do without them, because of the heat? Whatever the answer, if there was a pair of trousers, they were too short to stick out below the overall, so that the mayor looked as if he was wearing a nightshirt. More precisely – and the kind of skullcap that he wore on his head increased the impression – there was something medieval about him: you thought you had seen him somewhere before on a stained-glass window in a church.

'I don't suppose you need me, gentlemen?'

Standing in the doorway of the dusty room, Maigret and Mr Pyke looked at one another with some surprise, then looked at Lechat, and last of all at Félicien. On the table, the one, in fact, that was used for council meetings and elections, there was a white wooden coffin that looked as if it had seen better days.

As if it was the most natural thing in the world, Monsieur Jamet said to them, 'If you'd like to give me a hand, we'll put it back in the corner. It's the municipal coffin. We are obliged by law to supply the funerals of the poor and yet we only have one carpenter on the island, he's getting very old and he works slowly. In the summer, with the heat, the bodies can't wait.'

He talked about it as if it was an entirely everyday matter, and Maigret glanced at the man from Scotland Yard out of the corner of his eye.

'Do you have lots of poor people?'

'We have one, old Benoît.'

'So this coffin is meant for Benoît?'

'In principle. However, on Wednesday, it was used to transport Marcellin's body to Hyères. Don't worry. We disinfected it.'

The only places to sit in the room were some very comfortable folding chairs.

'Shall I leave you, gentlemen?'

'Just one moment. Who is Benoît?'

'You must have noticed him, or you will notice him: he has hair down to his shoulders and a shaggy beard. Hang on: through this window you can see him having a siesta on a bench, near the boules players.'

'Is he very old?'

'Nobody knows. Not even him. Listening to him, he's about a hundred, but he must be boasting. He has no papers. No one knows his exact name. He landed on the island a very long time ago, when Morin-Barbu, who keeps the café on the corner, was still a young man.'

'Where did he come from?'

'Nobody knows that either. From Italy, definitely. Most of them have come from Italy. You can usually tell from their accent whether they're from Genoa or somewhere near Naples, but Benoît has a language of his own, he isn't easy to understand.'

'Is he simple-minded?'

'I'm sorry?'

'Is he a bit mad?'

'He's as clever as a monkey. Today he looks like a patriarch. In a few days, as soon as the summer crowd arrive, he will shave his beard and his skull. He does that the same time every year. And he will start fishing for mordus.'

It all needed to be learned.

'Mordus?'

'Mordus are worms with very hard heads that you find in the sand near the sea. Fishermen prefer to use them over other bait because they stay on the hook. They're very expensive. All summer, Benoît fishes for mordus, in the water up to his thighs. He was a bricklayer as a young man. He built many of the houses on the island. Do you need anything else, gentlemen?'

Maigret hurried to open the window, to banish the smell of stuffiness and mildew: it must only have been aired on the 14th of July, when they took out the flags and chairs.

The inspector didn't really know what he was doing there. He had no desire whatsoever to move on to the interrogations. Why had he said yes when Inspector Lechat had suggested it to him? Out of cowardice, because of Mr Pyke? Isn't it normal, when starting an investigation, to question people? Isn't that what they do in England? Would he be taken seriously if he started roaming about the island like a man who has nothing else to do?

However, it was the island that interested him at that moment, not any particular individual. What the mayor had just said, for example, set in motion a whole series of thoughts that were still vague. These men, on little boats, coming and going along the coasts, perfectly at home, as if strolling along a boulevard! It didn't match the image one has of the sea. It seemed to him that here the sea was something intimate. A few miles from Toulon, you met people who had come from Genoa and Naples, quite naturally, some of them in a boat, fishing along the way. A bit like Marcellin. They stopped and if they felt at ease they stayed, perhaps writing home to ask their wife or fiancée to join them.

'Would you like me to bring them in one by one, chief? Who would you like to start with?'

He didn't care.

'I see young de Greef crossing the square with his girl-friend. Shall I go and get him?'

He was jostled and didn't dare to protest. He had the consolation of noting that his colleague was just as lethargic as he was.

'These witnesses that you're going to hear,' he asked, 'are they called in regularly?'

'Not at all. They come because they want to. They have the right to answer or not answer. Most of the time they prefer to answer, but they could also demand the presence of a lawyer.'

Word must have got around that the inspector was at the

town hall, because groups were forming in the square as they had that morning. Some distance away, under the eucalyptus trees, Lechat was engaged in an animated conversation with a couple, who finally followed him. A mimosa was growing just beside the door, and its sweet perfume mingled curiously with the smell of mildew that prevailed in the room.

'I suppose these things are done with more solemnity in your country?'

'Not always. Often, in the country or in small towns, the coroner's inquiry is held in the back room of a pub.'

De Greef looked all the more blond because his skin was as tanned as a native of Tahiti. The only clothes he wore were light-coloured shorts and espadrilles, while his companion had a pareo wrapped around her body.

'You wanted to speak to me?' he said suspiciously.

And Lechat replied, to reassure him, 'Come in! Detective Chief Inspector Maigret has to question everybody. It's routine.'

The Dutchman spoke French almost without an accent. He held a shopping net in his hand. Perhaps they had been on their way to buy provisions, at the Cooperative, when the inspector had stopped them.

'Have you been living on your boat for a long time?'

'Three years. Why?'

'Nothing. You're a painter, I was told? Do you sell your paintings?'

'When the opportunity presents itself.'

'Does it present itself often?'

'It's quite rare. I sold a canvas to Mrs Wilcox last week.'

'Do you know her well?'

'I got to know her here.'

Lechat came and spoke to Maigret in a low voice. He wanted to know if he could go and get Monsieur Émile, and the inspector nodded.

'What kind of person is she?'

'Mrs Wilcox? She's very funny.'

'Meaning?'

'Nothing. I may have met her in Montparnasse, because she passes through Paris every winter. We've discovered that we had friends in common.'

'You've spent time in Montparnasse?'

'I lived in Paris for a year.'

'With your boat?'

'We were moored at the Pont Marie.'

'Are you rich?'

'I haven't a cent.'

'Tell me, how old is your girlfriend, exactly?'

'Eighteen and a half.'

The girl, her hair in her face and her flesh moulded by the pareo, looked like a young savage, and she glared furiously at Maigret and Mr Pyke.

'You aren't married?'

'No.'

'Were her parents against the idea?'

'They know she lives with me.'

'For how long?'

'Two and a half years.'

'In other words she was barely sixteen when she became your lover?'

The word didn't shock either of them.

'Didn't her parents try to get her back?'

'They did try, several times. She came back.'

'So they gave up?'

'They prefer not to think about it any more.'

'What did you live on in Paris?'

'I sold a painting or a drawing from time to time. I had friends.'

'Friends who lent you money?'

'Sometimes. Other times I carried vegetables at Les Halles. And I also handed out advertising leaflets.'

'Did you already have plans to come to Porquerolles?'

'I didn't know the island existed.'

'Where were you going to go?'

'Anywhere, as long as it was sunny.'

'And where do you intend to go?'

'Further away.'

'To Italy?'

'Or elsewhere.'

'Did you know Marcellin?'

'He helped me to caulk my boat, which was letting in water.'

'Were you at the Arche de Noé on the night he died?'

'We're there almost every evening.'

'What were you doing?'

'Anna and I were playing chess.'

'Can I ask you, Monsieur de Greef, your father's profession?'

'He's a judge at the court in Groningen.'

'You don't know why Marcellin was killed?'

'I'm not curious about it.'

'Did he talk to you about me?'

'If he did, I wasn't listening.'

'Do you own a revolver?'

'Why would I?'

'You have nothing to tell me?'

'Nothing at all.'

'And what about you, mademoiselle?'

'Nothing, thank you.'

He called them back just as they were about to leave.

'One more question. Right now, do you have any money?'

'I told you, I sold a painting to Mrs Wilcox.'

'Have you been on board her yacht?'

'Several times.'

'Doing what?'

'What do people do on board yachts?'

'I don't know.'

Then de Greef said, with a hint of contempt, 'We drink. We drank. Is that all?'

Lechat couldn't have had to go far to find Monsieur Émile, because the two men were standing in a patch of shade, a short way away from the town hall. Monsieur Émile seemed older than his sixty-five years, and he gave an impression of extreme fragility, moving only cautiously, as if he was afraid he might break. He spoke quietly, saving the very last scraps of his energy.

'Come in, Monsieur Émile. We know each other already, don't we?'

As Justine's son squinted towards a chair, Maigret went on:

'You can sit down. Did you know Marcellin?'

'Very well.'

'Were you in regular contact with him? Since when?'

'I couldn't rightly say for how many years. My mother will remember exactly. Since Ginette's been working for us.'

There was a short silence. It was very funny. It was as if a bubble had just burst in the calm air of the room. Maigret and Mr Pyke looked at each other. What had Mr Pyke said when they were leaving Paris? He had mentioned Ginette. He had been amazed – discreetly, as in everything he did – that the inspector had not inquired into what had become of her.

And yet he didn't need do to any research, or resort to subterfuge. Very simply, from the first words onwards, it was Monsieur Émile who talked about this woman, whom Maigret had once sent to a sanatorium.

'You say she's working for you? Which means, I suppose, in one of your houses.'

'The one in Nice.'

'Just a moment, Monsieur Émile. I met her at Ternes about fifteen years ago, and she wasn't a young girl then. If I'm not mistaken, she was already past thirty, and tuberculosis wasn't taking years off her. Now she must be . . .'

'Between forty-five and fifty.'

And Monsieur Émile added very simply, 'She runs Les Sirènes, in Nice.'

It was better not to look at Mr Pyke, whose pout became as ironic as his good manners allowed. Hadn't Maigret blushed? At any rate, he was aware of being perfectly ridiculous.

Because previously he had played the new boy. After sending Marcellin to jail, he had dealt with Ginette and, as in a pulp novel, he had 'taken her off the streets' to put her in a sanatorium.

He saw her very clearly in his mind, so thin that one wondered how men might be tempted, with her feverish eyes and slack mouth.

He said to her, 'You need treatment, little one.'

And she answered meekly, 'Yes, please, inspector. It really isn't much fun!'

With a hint of impatience, Maigret now stared Monsieur Émile in the face and asked, 'Are you sure it's the same woman? At the time she was riddled with TB.'

'She's had treatment for several years.'

'Did she stay with Marcellin?'

'She hardly saw him, in fact. She's very busy. She used to send him a cheque from time to time. Not huge sums. He didn't need them.'

Monsieur Émile took a eucalyptus pastille from a little tin and sucked it seriously.

'Did he go and see her in Nice?'

'I don't think so. He's an odd fish.'

'Is Ginette in Nice at the moment?'

'She called us this morning from Hyères. She found out what happened from the papers. She's in Hyères to sort out the funeral.'

'Do you know where she's staying?'

'At the Hôtel des Palmes.'

'Were you at the Arche on the evening of the murder?'

'I called in for my herbal tea.'

'Did you leave before Marcellin?'

'Certainly. I never go to bed after ten.'

'Did you hear him talking about me?'

'Maybe. I wasn't paying attention. I'm a little hard of hearing.'

'What's your relationship with Charlot?'

'I know him, but I don't spend time with him.'

Monsieur Émile was clearly trying to explain something delicate.

'It's not the same world, do you see?'

'He's never worked for your mother?'

'He might have found her staff from time to time.'

'Was he above board?'

'I think so.'

'Did Marcellin find staff for you as well?'

'No. That wasn't his line.'

'You know nothing about it?'

'Nothing at all. I barely get involved in business these days. My health doesn't allow it.'

What did Mr Pyke think about all this? Were there Monsieur Émiles in England too?

'I might go and chat with your mother for a moment.'

'You would be more than welcome, inspector.'

Lechat was outside, this time in the company of a young man in white flannel trousers, a checked blue jacket and a yachtsman's cap.

'Monsieur Philippe de Moricourt,' he announced. 'He was just landing in his dinghy.'

'Would you like to talk to me, inspector?'

He was about thirty and, contrary to what might have been expected, he wasn't even good-looking.

'I presume this is just a formality?'

'Sit down.'

'Do I really have to? I hate sitting down.'

'Then stand. You're Mrs Wilcox's secretary?'

'Unpaid, of course. Let's say that I'm her guest, and that out of friendship I sometimes act as her secretary.'

'Is Mrs Wilcox writing her memoirs?'

'No. Why would you ask me that?'

'Does she personally deal with her whisky distillery?'

'Not in the slightest.'

'Do you write her personal letters?'

'I don't see what you're getting at.'

'Nothing at all, Monsieur Moricourt.'

'De Moricourt.'

'If you like. I'm just trying to get a clear idea of your work.'

'Mrs Wilcox isn't as young as she was.'

'Exactly.'

'I don't get it.'

'It doesn't matter. Tell me, Monsieur de Moricourt – that's right, isn't it? – where did you meet Mrs Wilcox?'

'Is this an interrogation?'

'It's whatever you'd like it to be.'

'Do I have to answer?'

'You can wait for me to call you in officially.'

'Do you see me as a suspect?'

'Everyone and no one is a suspect.'

The young man thought for a few moments then threw his cigarette out of the open door.

'I met her at the casino in Cannes.'

'A long time ago?'

'A little more than a year.'

'Are you a gambler?'

'I have been. That's how I lost my money.'

'Did you have a lot?'

'That question strikes me as indiscreet.'

'Have you worked in the past?'

'I worked for a minister's office.'

'I suppose he was a friend of your family?'

'How did you know?'

'Do you know young de Greef?'

'He's been on the yacht several times, and we've bought a painting from him.'

'Do you mean Mrs Wilcox bought a painting from him?'

'Exactly. Excuse me.'

'Did Marcellin go aboard the *North Star* as well?'

'Sometimes, yes.'

'As a guest?'

'It's hard to explain, inspector. Mrs Wilcox is a very generous person.'

'I'm sure she is.'

'She's interested in everything, particularly in this Mediterranean region, which she loves, and which is teeming with colourful characters. Marcellin was without a doubt one of those characters.'

'Was he given something to drink?'

'We give everybody something to drink.'

'Were you at the Arche on the night of the crime?'

'We were with the major.'

'Another colourful character, I imagine?'

'Mrs Wilcox knew him from before, in England. It's a refined relationship.'

'Did you drink champagne?'

'The major drinks only champagne.'

'Were all three of you quite merry?'

'We were quite correct.'

'Did Marcellin get involved in your group?'

'Everyone got more or less involved. You don't know Major Bellam yet?'

'I'm sure I will soon have the pleasure.'

'He's generosity personified. When he comes to the Arche . . .'

'And does he go there often?'

'Very much so. I was saying that he almost always bought drinks for everyone. He's been on the island for so long that he knows the children by their first name.'

'So Marcellin approached your table. He had a glass of champagne.'

'No. He hated champagne. He claimed it was a drink for girls. He was brought a bottle of white wine.'

'Did he sit down?'

'Of course.'

'Were there other people sitting at your table? Charlot, for example?'

'Of course.'

'Do you know his profession, if I can use the word?'

'He doesn't hide the fact that he's part of the under-world. He's a character too.'

'And he was invited on board as such?'

'I think, inspector, that there was no one on the island who wasn't invited.'

'Even Monsieur Émile?'

'Not him.'

'Why?'

'I don't know. I don't think we ever said a word to him. He's rather solitary.'

'And he doesn't drink.'

'Quite.'

'Because you drink a lot on the boat, don't you?'

'Sometimes. It's allowed though, isn't it?'

'Was Marcellin at your table when he started talking about me?'

'Probably. I don't remember exactly. He was telling stories, as usual, Mrs Wilcox liked to hear him telling stories. He talked about his years in jail.'

'He's never been in jail.'

'In that case he was making it up.'

'To amuse Mrs Wilcox. So he talked about jail. And I was part of the story? Was he drunk?'

'He was never entirely sober, particularly in the evening. Wait! He said he'd gone down because of a woman.'

'Ginette?'

'Perhaps. I think I remember that name. It's then, I think, that he claimed that you'd taken charge of her. Someone muttered, "Maigret is a cop like all the others." Excuse me.'

'It's all right. Go on.'

'That's all. Then he started singing your praises, saying you were his friend and that as far as he was concerned friendship was sacred. If I remember correctly Charlot teased him, and he got very worked up.'

'Can you tell me exactly how it ended?'

'It's difficult. It was late.'

'Who left first?'

'I don't know. Paul had locked the shutters a long time before. He was sitting at our table. We drank one last bottle. I think we left together.'

'Who?'

'The major left us in the square to go back to his villa. Charlot, who sleeps at the Arche, stayed. Mrs Wilcox and I headed for the landing stage, where we'd left the dinghy.'

'Did you have a sailor with you?'

'No. Usually we leave them on board. There was a strong mistral, and the sea was stormy. Marcellin suggested taking us.'

'So he was with you when you boarded the boat?'

'Yes. He stayed on land. He must have gone back to his shack.'

'In short, Mrs Wilcox and you were the last people to see him alive?'

'Apart from the murderer.'

'Did you have trouble getting back to the yacht?'

'How do you know?'

'You told me the sea was bad.'

'We arrived soaked, with twenty centimetres of water in the dinghy.'

'Did you go straight to bed?'

'I made some hot rums to warm us up, after which we had a game of gin rummy.'

'I'm sorry?'

'It's an English card game.'

'What time was it?'

'About two in the morning. We never go to bed early.'

'Did you see or hear anything unusual?'

'We couldn't hear anything because of the mistral.'

'Do you expect to go to the Arche this evening?'

'Probably.'

'Thank you.'

Maigret and Mr Pyke stayed on their own for a moment, and the inspector looked at his colleague with big drowsy eyes. He had a sense that it was all futile, that he should have started differently. For example, he would have liked to be in the square, in the sun, smoking his pipe and watching the boules players who had started a big game; he would have liked to roam in the port, watch the fishermen mending their nets; he would have liked to meet all the Gallis and Morins that Lechat had mentioned to him.

'I think, Mr Pyke, that in England investigations are carried out in a very orderly fashion, isn't that right?'

'It depends. For example, after a crime that was committed two years ago near Brighton, one of my colleagues spent eleven weeks in an inn, spending his days angling and his evenings drinking ale with the locals.'

It was exactly what Maigret would have liked to be doing, and which he wasn't doing because of that same Mr Pyke! By the time Lechat came in, he was in a bad mood.

'The major didn't want to come,' he announced. 'He's in his garden, doing nothing. I told him you were asking him to come here. He said that if you wanted to see him, you only had to go and have a bottle at his place.'

'That's his right.'

'Who do you want to question now?'

'No one. I'd like you to call Hyères. I suppose there is a phone, at the Arche? Ask for Ginette, at the Hôtel des Palmes. Tell her from me that I would be happy for her to come and chat to me.'

'Where will I find you?'

'I don't know. Probably at the harbour.'

They slowly crossed the square, he and Mr Pyke, and the people watched them as they walked. One might have imagined that they were watching suspiciously, but it was only because they didn't know how to approach the famous Maigret. For his part, Maigret felt like an 'estranger', the local word for outsiders. But he knew it wouldn't take much for them all to start talking with abandon, perhaps with too much abandon.

'Don't you think we have a sense of being very far away, Mr Pyke? Look! You can see France, over there, twenty minutes by boat, and I'm as disoriented as if I were in the heart of Africa or South America.'

Some children stopped playing to examine them. They reached the Grand Hôtel, discovered the harbour, and already Inspector Lechat was joining them.

'I couldn't get hold of her,' he announced. 'She left.'

'Has she gone back to Nice?'

'Probably not, because she told the landlord of the hotel

that she would be coming back the next morning, in time for the funeral.'

The jetty, the little boats of every colour, the big yacht blocking the harbour, the *North Star*, over near a rocky headland, and people watching another boat coming in.

'It's the *Cormoran*,' Lechat explained. 'In other words, it's nearly five o'clock.'

A boy in a cap bearing the words 'Grand Hôtel' in gold letters was waiting for potential customers beside a wheelbarrow intended for the luggage. The little white boat approached, the sea giving it a silvery moustache, and Maigret soon noticed, in the bow, a female outline.

'Probably Ginette, coming to meet us,' said Lechat. 'Everyone in Hyères must know you're here.'

It made a curious impression, seeing the figures on the boat growing gradually, coming into focus as if on a photographic plate. It was particularly disturbing to see Ginette's features on a very fat, very dignified woman, all in silk, in full make-up and probably highly perfumed.

In fact, when Maigret had known her at the Brasserie des Ternes, had he too not been slimmer, and might she not be feeling the same disappointment as he did, watching him from the deck of the *Cormoran*?

She had to be helped off the boat. Apart from her there was no one on board but Baptiste, the captain, the silent sailor and the postman. The boy with the braided cap wanted to take charge of the luggage.

'To the Arche de Noé!' she said.

She came towards Maigret and then hesitated, perhaps because of Mr Pyke, whom she didn't know.

'I was told you were here. I thought you'd like to talk to me. Poor Marcel . . .!'

She didn't say Marcellin, like the others. She didn't put on a display of grief. She had become a mature person, comfortable and calm, with a hint of a disillusioned smile.

'Are you staying at the Arche too?'

It was Lechat who took her suitcase. She seemed to know the island and walked calmly, without haste, like a person who gets easily out of breath, or who is not made for the great outdoors.

'According to what I read in *Le Petit Var*, it's because he talked about you that he was killed. Do you believe that?'

From time to time she glanced curiously and uneasily at Mr Pyke.

'You can speak in front of him. He's a friend, an English colleague who's come to spend a few days with me.'

She gave the man from Scotland Yard the little wave of a very worldly woman and sighed with a glance at Maigret's thick waist.

'I've changed, haven't I?'

4. Ginette's Engagement

It was strange to see her making a modest gesture and holding her dress tightly to her because the stairs were steep and Maigret was climbing behind her.

She had stepped into the Arche as if she were right at home, and had said very naturally, 'Do you still have a room for me, Paul?'

'You will have to make do with the little room beside the bathroom.'

Then she turned towards Maigret.

'Won't you come up for a moment, inspector?'

Her words might have had a double meaning in the house she ran in Nice, but not here. But she misunderstood the hesitation on the part of Maigret, who still prided himself on hiding nothing about the investigation from Mr Pyke. For a moment she wore an almost professional smile.

'I won't bite, you know.'

Amazingly, the inspector from Scotland Yard spoke in English, perhaps out of delicacy. He said only one word to his French colleague: 'Please . . .'

On the stairs, Jojo walked ahead with the suitcase. She was wearing a very short skirt, and they glimpsed the pink underwear that covered her little bottom. That was probably what had prompted Ginette to hold her dress against her.

Apart from the bed, the only place to sit was a straw-bottomed chair, because this was the smallest of the rooms, dimly lit by a skylight. Ginette took her hat off, slumped on the edge of the bed with a sigh of relief and immediately took off her very high-heeled shoes, stroking her painful toenails through the silk of her stockings.

'Are you annoyed that I asked you to come up? There's no way of talking downstairs, and I couldn't face walking. Look at my ankles: they're swollen. You can smoke your pipe, inspector.'

She wasn't completely at ease. There was a sense that she was speaking for the sake of it, to gain some time.

'Are you very angry with me?'

Even though he had understood, he too gained some time, replying, 'For what?'

'I'm well aware that you've been disappointed. And yet it isn't really my fault. Thanks to you, I spent the happiest years of my life at the sanatorium. I didn't have to worry about anything. There was a doctor who looked a bit like you and who was very kind to me. He brought me books. I read all day. Before I went there, I was ignorant. Then, when there was something I didn't understand, he explained it to me. Have you got a cigarette? Doesn't matter. Besides, it's better if I don't smoke . . .

'I spent five years at the sanatorium and in the end I thought I would spend the rest of my life there. I enjoyed it. Unlike the others, I didn't want to leave.

'When I was told that I was cured and could leave, I swear I was more apprehensive than relieved. From where we were, you could see the valley, almost always covered in light fog, sometimes in thick clouds, and I was frightened of going back down. I would have liked to stay as a nurse but I didn't have the necessary knowledge and I wasn't strong enough to do the housework or be a kitchen maid.

'What could I have done down there? I was used to having three meals a day. I knew I would find that at Justine's.'

'Why did you come today?' Maigret asked in a rather frosty voice.

'Didn't I just tell you that? I went to Hyères first. I didn't want poor Marcel to be buried with no one behind the hearse.'

'Did you still love him?'

She paused awkwardly for a moment.

'You know, I think I did. I used to talk to you about him back when you were interested in me, after he was arrested. He wasn't a bad fellow, you know? Basically he was a bit of an innocent, I'd even go so far as to say that he was timid. And precisely because he was timid he wanted to be like the others. Except that he overdid it. Up there, I worked it all out.'

'And you didn't love him any more.'

'Not in the same way. I saw other people. I was able to make comparisons. The doctor helped me to understand.'

'Were you in love with the doctor?'

She gave a slightly nervous laugh.

'I think that in a sanatorium you're always more or less in love with your doctor.'

'Did Marcel write to you?'

'From time to time.'

'Did he hope to resume his life with you?'

'At first, I think so, yes. Then he changed as well. The two of us didn't change in the same way. He aged very quickly, almost all at once. I don't know if you saw him again. He used to dress smartly, he looked after himself. He was proud. It all started when he came to the Côte d'Azur, by chance.'

'Did he put you to work for Justine and Émile?'

'No. I just knew Justine by name. I introduced myself to her. She employed me on a trial basis, as a madam's assistant, because I wasn't fit for anything else. I had four operations up there, and my body is covered with scars.'

'I asked you why you came today.'

He kept insistently returning to this question.

'When I knew you were in charge of the case, I thought you'd remember me and have people look for me. It would probably have taken some time.'

'If I understand correctly, since leaving the sanatorium you haven't had a relationship with Marcel, but you used to send him cheques?'

'Sometimes. I wanted him to enjoy himself a little. He didn't let it show, but he went through some hard times.'

'Did he tell you that?'

'He told me he was a failure, that he had always been a failure, that he wasn't even up to being a real villain.'

'Did he tell you that in Nice?'

'He never came to see me at Les Sirènes. He knew it was forbidden.'

'Here?'

'Yes.'

'Do you come to Porquerolles often?'

'Every month, more or less. Justine is too old to inspect her houses herself. Monsieur Émile has never liked travelling.'

'Do you stay here, at the Arche?'

'Always.'

'Why doesn't Justine give you a room at hers? The villa is spacious enough.'

'She never lets a woman sleep under her roof.'

Maigret felt that he was getting to the heart of the matter, but Ginette hadn't yet given up completely.

'Does she fear for her son?' he joked, lighting a new pipe.

'It might sound funny, but it's the truth. She has tied him to her apron-strings, and that's why he's ended up more like a girl than a boy. At his age, she still treats him like a child. He can't do anything without her permission.'

'Does he like women?'

'He's rather afraid of them. I mean in general. It's not really his thing, you know? He's never been in good health. He spends his time caring for himself, taking drugs, reading medical books.'

'What else is there, Ginette?'

'What do you mean?'

'Why did you come today?'

'I've told you that.'

'No.'

'I thought you'd be taking a close look at Monsieur Émile and his mother.'

'Tell me more.'

'You're not like the other policemen, but still! When

something bad happens, suspicion always falls on people from a particular milieu.'

'And are you telling me that Monsieur Émile has nothing to do with Marcel's death?'

'I wanted to explain to you . . .'

'Explain what to me?'

'We've stayed good friends, Marcel and I, but there was no question of us living together. He wouldn't even have thought of it now. I don't think he wanted to. Do you understand? He liked the kind of life he'd made for himself. He'd fallen out of contact with that set. Hang on! I spotted Charlot, just now . . .'

'Do you know him?'

'I've met him here several times. Sometimes we've dined at the same table. He used to find women for me.'

'Did you expect him to be in Porquerolles today?'

'No. I swear I'm telling you the truth. It's your way of asking questions that's putting me off. You used to trust me. You pitied me a little. It's true, I don't have anything left to be pitied for, do I? I'm not even tubercular these days!'

'Do you make a lot of money?'

'Not as much as you might imagine. Justine is very stingy. So is her son. Obviously I lack nothing. I even put a little aside, but not enough to live on when I retire.'

'You were talking to me about Marcel.'

'I can't remember what I was saying. Oh, yes! How to explain it? When you knew him, he was trying to be a hard man. In Paris he went to the kind of bars where you meet people like Charlot or even hired killers. He wanted to look as if he was part of their gangs, and they didn't take him seriously . . .'

'He was a bit of a softy?'

'Well, it suited him. He stopped seeing those people and lived on his boat or in his shack. He drank a lot. He always found the money to get hold of a drop. My cheques helped. I know what people think when a man like him is killed . . .'

'Meaning?'

'You know as well as I do. It would be easy to think it's a mob thing, a settling of scores, or an act of revenge. But it's not the case.'

'That was what you wanted to tell me, wasn't it?'

'I lost track of my thoughts a few minutes ago. You've changed so much! Forgive me. I don't mean physically.'

He smiled in spite of his embarrassment.

'Before, even in your office on Quai des Orfèvres, you didn't seem like a policeman.'

'Are you very worried about me suspecting people from the criminal milieu? You're not in love with Charlot, by any chance?'

'Certainly not. I'd have trouble being in love with anyone after all the operations I've had. I'm no longer a woman, if you must know. And Charlot doesn't interest me more than anyone else.'

'Tell me the rest now.'

'Why do you think there's more to come? I give you my word of honour that I don't know who could have killed poor Marcel.'

'But you know who didn't.'

'Yes.'

'You know who I might be led to suspect.'

'After all, you'll find out anyway one of these days, if you haven't found out already. I would have told you from the start if you hadn't questioned me so brusquely. I have to marry Monsieur Émile, and there you have it!'

'When?'

'When Justine dies.'

'Why do you have to wait until she's not around?'

'I'll say it again: she's jealous of all women. It's because of her that he has never married and that he's never had lovers. When, once in a blue moon, he needed a woman, it was his mother who chose the least dangerous one for him, and she never stopped making recommendations to him. Now that's all over.'

'For whom?'

'For him, of course!'

'And yet he's planning to get married?'

'Because he's terrified of ending up on his own. While his mother's alive, he's fine. She looks after him like a baby. But she hasn't got long to go. A year at most.'

'Is that what the doctor says?'

'She has cancer, and she's too old to survive an operation. As for him, he's forever thinking that he's going to die. He gets breathless several times a day, I don't dare to touch him, as if the slightest movement could be fatal for him . . .'

'So that's why he suggested you marry him?'

'Yes. He's checked that I'm in good enough health to look after him. He's even had me examined by several doctors. I don't need to tell you that Justine doesn't know anything, because she'd have thrown me out long ago.'

'And Marcel?'

'I told him.'

'How did he react?'

'He didn't. He thought I was right to make plans for my old age. I think he was pleased to know that I was going to come and live here.'

'Was Monsieur Émile jealous of Marcel?'

'Why would he have been jealous? I've already told you there was nothing between us.'

'So in short, that's what you were so keen to talk to me about?'

'I've thought about all the assumptions you would make, which have nothing to do with reality.'

'For example, that Marcel might have blackmailed Monsieur Émile, and that Monsieur Émile, to get rid of him . . .'

'Marcel didn't blackmail anyone, and Monsieur Émile would rather die than wring the neck of a chicken.'

'Of course, you hadn't been on the island over the past few days?'

'It's easy to check.'

'Because you haven't left the house in Nice, have you? It's an excellent alibi.'

'Do I need one?'

'According to what you said just now, I talk like a policeman. Marcel, in spite of everything, could have got in your way. Particularly since Monsieur Émile is a big fish, a very big fish. Assuming that he marries you, he would leave you a serious fortune when he died.'

'Quite serious, yes! Now I wonder if I did the right thing in coming here. I didn't imagine that you would talk to me like that. I've confessed everything to you, quite honestly.'

Her eyes were glistening as if she were about to cry, and the face that Maigret found himself contemplating looked badly replastered and clouded by a childish pout.

'You'll do as you see fit. I don't know who killed Marcel. It's a disaster.'

'Particularly for him.'

'For him too, yes. But he's at peace. Are you going to arrest me?'

She said that with a hint of a smile, even though it was plain that she was anxious, and more serious than she wished to appear.

'I don't plan to for the moment.'

'Will I be able to go to the funeral tomorrow morning? If you like I'll come back straight afterwards. You'll just have to send a boat to the Giens headland to pick me up.'

'Maybe.'

'You won't say anything to Justine?'

'No more than strictly necessary, and I don't foresee that necessity.'

'Are you angry with me?'

'Not at all.'

'Yes, you are. I sensed it straight away, before I got off the *Cormoran*, as soon as I spotted you. I recognized you. I was moved, because it was a whole part of my life coming back to me.'

'A part that you regret?'

'Perhaps. I don't know. Sometimes I wonder.'

She got up with a sigh, without putting her shoes back on. She wanted to unlace her corset and she was waiting for the inspector to leave so that she could.

'You do what you like,' she sighed at last, as he held out his hand towards the door handle.

And he felt something clenching in his heart as he left her all on her own, old and anxious, in the little room where the setting sun came in through the skylight, bathing everything, the wallpaper on the walls and the counterpane, in a pink the colour of blusher.

'A glass of white wine, Monsieur Maigret!'

Noise, all of a sudden, and movement. The boules players, who had finished their game in the square, surrounded the bar, speaking very loudly in a strong accent. In a corner of the dining room, near the window, Mr Pyke was sitting at the table opposite Jef de Greef, and the two men were deeply absorbed in a game of chess.

Beside them, on the banquette, sat Anna, smoking a cigarette in a long cigarette-holder. She had got dressed. She wore a little cotton dress, under which she was clearly as naked as she had been under the pareo. Her flesh was heavy and very feminine, so plainly made for caresses that one couldn't help imagining her in bed.

De Greef had put on grey flannel trousers and a blue-and-white striped sailor's jersey. On his feet he wore rope-soled espadrilles, like almost everyone on the island, and they were the first thing that the very strict Mr Pyke had bought.

Maigret looked around for the Lechat but didn't see

him. He had no choice but to accept the glass of wine that Paul was pushing towards him, and the people at the bar crowded together to make room for him.

'So, inspector?'

He was being addressed and he knew that in a few minutes the ice would have melted. Wasn't it likely that since that morning the islanders had been waiting for this moment to make his acquaintance? There were quite a lot of them, ten at least, most of them wearing fishermen's clothes. Two or three others looked more well-to-do, perhaps small property-owners.

Whatever Mr Pyke thought about it, he had to drink.

'You like our wine from the island?'

'A lot.'

'And yet the papers say you only drink beer. Marcellin said there was no truth in it, that you wouldn't turn your nose up at a bottle of calvados. Poor Marcellin! Your health, inspector . . .'

Paul, the landlord, who knew how these things work, kept the bottle in his hand.

'Is it true that he was your friend?'

'I used to know him, yes. He wasn't a bad fellow.'

'Certainly not. Is it also true, what they're saying in the papers, that he came from Le Havre?'

'Indeed it is.'

'With his accent?'

'When I knew him fifteen years ago he didn't have an accent.'

'You hear that, Titin? What have I always told you?'

Four rounds . . . five rounds . . . and words being thrown

about rather at random, like children throwing balls in the air.

'What would you like to eat this evening, inspector? There's bouillabaisse, of course. But perhaps you don't like bouillabaisse?'

He swore that it was his favourite, and everyone was enchanted. It wasn't a good moment, given the confused mass of people surrounding him, to strike up personal acquaintances.

'You like pastis, too, the real one, the one that's forbidden? A round of pastis, Paul! Of course! The inspector won't say anything . . .'

Charlot was sitting on the terrace, over a pastis, in fact, busy reading a paper.

'Do you have an idea already?'

'An idea of what?'

'Who the murderer is! Morin-Barbu, who was born on the island and hasn't left it for seventy-seven years, has never heard of anything like it. People have drowned. A woman from the North, five or six years ago, tried to take her own life with sleeping pills. An Italian sailor stabbed Baptiste in the arm in an argument. But a crime? Never, inspector! Even the bad people here become meek as lambs.'

Everyone was laughing and trying to talk, because what counted was talking, saying the first thing that came into their head, clinking glasses with the famous detective chief inspector.

'You'll have a better idea when you've been here for a few days. What you need to do is come and spend your holidays here with your lady companion. We'll teach you to play boules. Won't we, Casimir? Casimir won the Petit Provençal competition last year, and you must know what that means.'

From the pink it had been a moment before, the church at the end of the square was assuming a purple colour; the sky was gently turning pale green, and the men were leaving one after the other; sometimes the shrill voice of a woman could be heard calling in the distance:

'Hey! Jules . . . Soup's on the table . . .'

Or a little boy came dutifully to look for his father and take him by the hand.

'So shall we have that game?'

'It's too late.'

They explained to Maigret that after the game of boules came the game of cards, but that it wasn't going to happen because he was there. The sailor of the *Cormoran*, a mute colossus with vast bare feet, gave the inspector a toothy smile and, from time to time, holding out his glass, emitted a strange gulping noise that seemed to mean 'cheers!'

'Do you want to have dinner straight away?'

'Have you seen the inspector?'

'He went out when you were up there. He didn't say anything. That's his way. He's famous, did you know? He's been ferreting around on the island for three days and knows almost as much as I do about all the families.'

Leaning forwards, Maigret saw that de Greef and his girlfriend had left, and that the Englishman was alone with his game of chess.

'We'll eat in half an hour,' he announced.

Paul asked him in a low voice, pointing to the inspector from Scotland Yard: 'Do you think he likes our cooking?'

A few minutes later Maigret and his colleague were walking, quite naturally, towards the harbour. They had caught the habit. The sun was down, and the atmosphere was one of immense relaxation. The sounds were no longer the same. Now you could hear the faint lapping of the water against the sound of the jetty, and those stones had turned a harsher grey; like the cliffs. The vegetation was dark, almost black, mysterious, and a torpedo-boat with a big number painted in white on its bow slipped silently towards the high seas at what looked like dizzying speed.

'I only just beat him,' Mr Pyke had said at first. 'He's very good, he's very much in control of himself.'

'Did he suggest playing?'

'I'd taken the chessboard to practise,' (he didn't add: 'while you were upstairs with Ginette'), 'not hoping to find a partner. He sat down at the next table with his companion, and I understood, from the way he looked at the pieces, that he wanted to test himself against me.'

After that there had been a long silence, and now the two men were advancing along the jetty. Near the white yacht there was a little boat whose name could be seen on the stern: *Fleur d'amour*.

It was de Greef's boat, and the couple were on board. There was, in fact, a light on under the roof, in a cabin just big enough for two people, too low to stand up in. The sound of spoons and dishes came from it. They were eating.

When the policemen had passed the yacht, Mr Pyke spoke again, slowly, with his usual precision.

'He's exactly the kind of boy they hate to have in good families. It's true that you mustn't have many such specimens in France.'

Maigret was very surprised, because it was the first time since he had known him that his colleague had come out with any kind of generalization. Mr Pyke himself seemed slightly embarrassed, as if modesty had got the better of him.

'What makes you think we don't have many of them in France?'

'I mean of that precise variety.'

He started searching for his words very carefully, stopping at the end of the jetty, facing the mountains that they could see on the mainland.

'I think that where you come from a boy from a good family can do stupid things, as you say, living the high life, spending money on women or cars, or gambling in casinos. Do your ne'er-do-wells play chess? I doubt it. Do they read Kant, Schopenhauer, Nietzsche and Kierkegaard? Unlikely, isn't it? They just want to live their lives without waiting for their inheritance.'

They leaned against the wall that ran along one side of the jetty; the calm surface of the water was sometimes troubled by a jumping fish.

'De Greef doesn't belong to this category of ne'er-do-wells. I don't even think he wants to own money. He's an almost pure anarchist. He has rebelled against everything he has known, everything he has been taught, against his father the magistrate and his mother the middle-class matron, against his town, against the customs of his country—'

He broke off, almost blushing.

'Forgive me . . .'

'Go on, please.'

'He and I only exchanged a few phrases, but I think I understood, because there are lots of young people like him in my country, probably in every country where morals are rigid. That's why I said just now that I suspect one doesn't meet huge numbers of such people in France. There's no hypocrisy here. Perhaps there isn't enough.'

Was he alluding to the milieu in which they had been wading since their arrival, the Monsieur Émiles, the Charlots, the Ginettes, who lived among the rest without being visibly marked by opprobrium?

Maigret was slightly concerned, slightly tense. Without being attacked, he felt a vague desire to defend himself.

'Out of protest,' Mr Pyke went on, 'those young people reject everything wholesale, the good and the bad. Look! He's abducted a little girl from her family. She's nice, very desirable. But I don't think he's done it out of desire for her. It's because she belonged to a good family, because she was a girl who went to mass on Sunday with her mother. It's because her father is probably an austere and respectable gentleman. It's also probably because he risked a lot in abducting her. I might be wrong, mightn't I?'

'I don't think so.'

'There are people who, in a clean and elegant setting, feel the need to sully it. De Greef feels a need to sully life, to sully anything. And even to sully his companion.'

This time Maigret was stunned, dumbfounded, because he understood that Mr Pyke had thought the same thing as he had. When de Greef had admitted having been on board the *North Star* several times, he had immediately found himself thinking that he hadn't gone there only to drink, but that there had been more intimate and less respectable relations between the two couples.

'They are very dangerous young men,' Mr Pyke concluded.

He added: 'Perhaps they're also very unhappy?'

Then, probably finding the silence a little too solemn, he said in a lighter tone:

'He speaks perfect English, you know. He doesn't even have an accent. I wouldn't be surprised if he had even passed through one of our great colleges.'

It was time to go to dinner. The half-hour was well passed. The darkness was almost complete, and the boats in the harbour bobbed to the rhythm of the sea's breathing. Maigret tapped his pipe on his heel to empty it and hesitated to fill another one. In passing, he looked intently at the Dutchman's boat.

Had Mr Pyke just been talking for the sake of talking? Had he been trying, in his way, to pass on some sort of message to him?

It was difficult, if not impossible, to know. His French was perfect, too perfect, and yet the two men didn't speak the same language, their thoughts travelled differently along the meanders of the brain.

'They are very dangerous young men,' the inspector from Scotland Yard had emphasized.

In all likelihood he wouldn't have wanted even to seem as if he was intervening in Maigret's investigation. He hadn't asked him any questions about what had happened in Ginette's room. Did he imagine that his colleague was hiding something from him, that Maigret was trying to hoodwink him? Or worse, after what he had just said about the morals of the French, did he imagine that Maigret and Ginette . . .?

Maigret muttered, 'She told me she was getting engaged to Monsieur Émile. It has to stay a secret, because of old Justine, who would try to prevent the marriage, even from beyond the grave.'

He realized that in comparison with Mr Pyke's incisive sentences his speech was vague, and his ideas still more so.

In a few words, the Englishman had said what he had to say. From half an hour spent with de Greef, he had drawn precise ideas not only about the man himself, but about the world in general.

Maigret would have had trouble expressing a single idea. He was completely different. He sensed something. He sensed a lot of things, as he always did at the start of an investigation, but he couldn't have said how that fog of ideas would sooner or later end up clearing.

It was a little humiliating. It lacked prestige. He felt heavy and soft beside his colleague's sharp outline.

'She's a funny girl,' he murmured, none the less.

That was all he could find to say about someone he had met before, someone about whom he knew practically everything and who had opened her heart to him.

A funny girl! Some aspects of her attracted him, others disappointed him, as she had clearly sensed.

Perhaps he would have a definitive idea about her later on?

After just one game of chess and a few words exchanged over the pieces, Mr Pyke had provided a definitive analysis of his partner's character.

Wasn't it as if the Englishman had won the first round?

5. Night in the Arche

He had noticed the smell first of all, when he still thought he was about to go to sleep straight away. In fact there were several smells. The main one, the smell of the house, the one that hit you immediately after crossing the threshold of the café, was one that he had been trying to analyse since that morning, because it was a smell that he wasn't familiar with. It struck him every time he came in and, each time, he wrinkled his nostrils. There was, of course, a ground note of wine, with a hint of aniseed and then some hints of cooking. And since it was Mediterranean cooking, based on garlic, red pepper, oil and saffron, he couldn't quite place it.

But what was the point of thinking about such things? With his eyes closed, he tried to get to sleep. There was no point remembering all the Marseillais or Provençal restaurants where he had eaten, in Paris or elsewhere. The smell wasn't the same anyway. All he needed to do was go to sleep. He had drunk enough to slip into the deepest slumber.

Hadn't he gone to sleep just after going to bed? The window was open, and a sound had intrigued him; he had finally worked out that it was the rustling of the leaves of the trees in the square.

At a pinch, the smell from below might be compared to

that of a little bar in Cannes, with a fat landlady, where had worked on a case in the past and where he had spent many lazy hours.

The smell in the room wasn't like anything else. What was there in the mattresses? Was it, as in Brittany, kelp, which gave off the iodine smell of the sea? Other people had been in this bed before him, and occasionally he thought he recognized the smell of that oil that women spread on their bodies when they go sunbathing.

He turned over heavily. It was at least the tenth time, and there was still someone opening a door, walking along the corridor and going to the toilet. There was nothing unusual about that, but it seemed to him that there were many more people in the corridor than were actually staying in the hotel. So he started counting the occupants of the Arche. Paul and his wife were sleeping overhead, in an attic room reached by a kind of ladder. As to Jojo, he didn't know where she slept. At any rate, there was no room for her on the first floor.

She too had a smell that was all her own. Part of it came from her oiled hair, part from her body and her clothes, and it was both muted and spicy, not disagreeable. The smell had distracted him while she was talking to him.

Another instance where Mr Pyke might have thought that Maigret was hoodwinking him. The inspector had gone up to his room for a moment after dinner to brush his teeth and wash his hands. He had left the door open, and silently, without the sound of footsteps on the floor, Jojo had come and stood in the doorway. How old was she? Sixteen, perhaps? Twenty? She had the expression, both admiring and fearful, of those young girls who wait for autographs by stage doors. She was impressed by Maigret because he was famous.

'Is there something you want to say to me, my dear?'

She had closed the door behind her, which he hadn't liked because you never know what people will think. He hadn't forgotten that there was an Englishman in the building.

'It's about Marcellin,' she said, blushing. 'He talked to me one afternoon when he was very drunk and having a siesta on the banquette in the café.'

Hang on! Just now, when the Arche was empty, he had seen someone lying on that same banquette with a newspaper over his head, enjoying a little snooze. It was clearly nice and cool there. A funny hotel all the same! As to the smell . . .

'I thought that might be useful to you. He told me that if he wanted, he could have a packet that fat.'

'A packet of what?'

'Banknotes, I'm pretty sure.'

'A long time ago?'

'I think it was two days before the thing that happened.'

'There wasn't anyone else in the café?'

'I was alone, polishing the bar.'

'Did you talk to anyone about it?'

'I don't think so.'

'He didn't say anything else?'

'Just: "What would I do with it, little Jojo? We're fine here as it is."'

'He never came on to you, there were no propositions?'

'No.'

'And what about the others?'

'Nearly all of them.'

'When Ginette was here – because she came here almost every month, didn't she? – Marcellin never went up to see her in her room?'

'Definitely not. He was very respectful of her.'

'Can I talk to you as a grown-up, Jojo?'

'I'm nineteen, you know.'

'Fine. Did Marcellin have relationships with women from time to time?'

'Of course.'

'On the island?'

'With Nina, first of all. She's my cousin. She goes with everyone. Apparently she can't help it.'

'Aboard his boat?'

'Anywhere at all. Then with the widow Lambert, who keeps the café on the other side of the square. He sometimes spent the night at hers. When he was fishing for sea bass, he would bring them to her. I suppose that now he's dead I can say it: Marcellin fished with dynamite.'

'There was never any question of him marrying the widow Lambert?'

'I don't think she wants to remarry.'

And Jojo's smile gave him to understand that the widow Lambert was no ordinary character.

'Is that all, Jojo?'

'Yes. I should go back down.'

Ginette wasn't sleeping either. She was lying in the bedroom next door, just behind the partition wall, so that

Maigret thought he could hear her breathing. That was awkward for him, because when he turned over in his half-sleep he sometimes knocked the wall with his elbow, and that must have given her a start every time he did so.

It had taken her a long time before going to bed: what could she have been doing? Beauty treatments, washing? The silence was sometimes so complete in her room that Maigret wondered if she mightn't be writing something. Particularly since the skylight was too high for her to be able to lean on it and catch some air.

To come back to that smell . . . It was, quite simply, the smell of Porquerolles. He had inhaled it, partly, at the end of the jetty, just now with Mr Pyke. There were exhalations that came from the water, overheated by the sun during the day, and others that came from the earth, on the breeze. Weren't the trees in the square eucalyptuses? There were probably other perfumed essences on the island.

Who was that in the corridor this time? Mr Pyke? It was the third time. Paul's cooking, for which he was so unprepared, must have disturbed him.

Mr Pyke had drunk a lot. Was it because he liked it or because he couldn't help himself? In any case, he liked champagne, and Maigret had never thought to offer him any. He had drunk it all evening with the major. The two men had got on so well that one would have thought they had known each other for ever. They had settled in a corner. Jojo had brought the champagne on her own initiative.

Bellam didn't drink it from coupes, but from big glasses, as if it was beer. He was so perfect that he looked like a

85

drawing of Mr Punch, with his silvery hair, his pink complexion, his big pale eyes floating in liquid and the huge cigar that never left his lips.

He was a child of seventy or seventy-two, with a flicker of mischief in his eye. Even after several bottles he maintained a winning dignity.

'Allow me to introduce Major Bellam,' Mr Pyke had said eventually. 'As it happens, we studied at the same college.'

Not in the same year, certainly, or even the same decade. It was clear that they were both delighted. The major called the chief inspector 'M'sieur Maigrette'.

From time to time he gave a barely perceptible sign to Jojo or Paul, which was enough for them to bring fresh champagne to the table. At other times, a different sign summoned Jojo, who filled a glass and went to bring it to someone in the bar.

There could have been something lofty or condescending about it. The major did it so nicely, so naively, that no one found it awkward. He looked a little as if he were distributing good marks. When the glass had reached its destination, he raised his own in a silent, distant toast.

Everyone, or almost, passed through the place. Charlot had been on the claw machine almost all evening. First he had played the fruit machine, and he could afford to put in as much as he liked, because in the end he was the one who collected the kitty. The claw machine must have belonged to him as well. He slipped the coin into the slot, then with sustained attention he turned the button that directed the little chrome pincer towards a cigarette box worth a few cents, or a pipe, or a wallet from a general store.

Was it anxiety that was keeping Ginette awake? Had Maigret been too mean to her? In her room, yes, he had been harsh. Not out of spite, as one might have thought. Had she thought it was out of spite?

It is always ridiculous, playing the Good Samaritan. He had picked her up on Place des Ternes and sent her to the sanatorium. He had never said to himself that he was saving a soul, that he was 'taking a girl off the streets'.

Someone else, someone 'who looked like him', as she had put it, had looked after her in turn: the sanatorium doctor. Had he hoped for something in return?

She had become what she had become. It was her affair. He had no reason to be annoyed about it, to feel any bitterness.

He had been harsh because you have to be, because such women, even the best of them, lie as easily as breathing, sometimes when they don't have to, sometimes for no reason. And she hadn't yet told him everything, he was sure of it. It was so true that she couldn't get to sleep. Something was troubling her.

Once she got up. He heard her bare feet on the floor of the bedroom. Was she coming to see him? It wasn't impossible, and Maigret had mentally prepared himself to hurry and put on his trousers, which he had dropped on the rug.

She hadn't come. There had been a clink of glass. She was thirsty. Or else she had taken a sleeping pill.

He had had only one glass of champagne. The rest of the time he had mostly drunk wine and then, God knows why, anisette.

Who had ordered anisette? Oh, yes! It was the dentist.

A former dentist, more precisely, whose name escaped him. Another freak. There were only freaks on the island, or at the Arche at any rate. Or perhaps they were the ones who were right, while the others, on the mainland, were wrong to behave differently?

He must have been a very fine, very elegant man, because he had a dental surgery in one of the smartest areas of Bordeaux, and the Bordelais are very hard to please. He had come to Porquerolles by chance, on holiday, and since then he had only been away for a week, long enough to sell off his business.

He didn't wear a false collar. He had his hair cut once a month by one of the Morins, a fisherman. That particular Morin was called 'Morin the Barber'. The former dentist had at least three days' growth of beard, he didn't take care of his hands, he no longer took care of anything, he did nothing but read, in a rocking chair, in the shade of his veranda.

He had married a girl from the island who might once have been pretty, but who had very quickly become enormous, with the hint of a moustache on her upper lip and a screeching voice.

He was happy. Or at least he claimed to be. He said with worrying assurance:

'You see! If you stay for a certain amount of time you will be bitten, like the others. And then you will never leave.'

Maigret knew that on certain Pacific islands white men sometimes let themselves go, 'went native', as they said over there, but he hadn't known it was possible three miles off the coast of France.

When you mentioned someone to the dentist, he judged him only according to his degree of 'going native'. He didn't call it that. He said: porquerollitis.

The doctor? Because there was also a doctor, whom Maigret hadn't yet met, but whom Lechat had spoken to him about. According to the dentist he had caught it badly.

'I assume you're friends?'

'We never see each other. We say hello to each other, from a distance.'

The doctor had, it was true, made certain preparations upon his arrival. He was very ill and had only settled on the island to cure himself. He was a bachelor. He lived alone in a cabin with a garden full of flowers and did all his own housekeeping. His house was very dirty. Because of his health he didn't go out in the evening, not even in an emergency, and in the winter, if it happened to be really cold, which was rare, you could spend days and sometimes weeks without seeing his white nose.

'You'll see! You'll see!' the dentist insisted with a sarcastic smile. 'Besides, you already have an idea of what it's like by looking around you. Just realize that it's the same thing every evening.'

And in fact it was a strange spectacle. It wasn't quite the atmosphere of a café, but neither was it that of someone's drawing room. The untidiness made it more like a soirée in an artist's studio.

Everyone knew everyone else, and no one pushed the boat out for anyone else. The major, who had been at a great English college, was on the same footing here as a dock rat like Marcellin, or a Charlot.

Every now and again someone changed places, or partners.

At first Monsieur Émile and Ginette had stayed calmly and silently at the same table, near the bar, like an old married couple waiting for a train at a station. Monsieur Émile had ordered his usual herb tea, and Ginette a green-ish liqueur in a tiny glass. Sometimes they exchanged a word or two, in an undertone. It was impossible to hear anything. You could only see the movement of their lips. Then Ginette had risen to her feet with a sigh and gone to get a game of draughts from a drawer under the record player.

They played. You had a sense that it might have been like that every day, for many years, that people could age without moving from the spot, without trying out any gestures other than the ones they were seen to be making.

Wasn't it likely that in five years Maigret would find the dentist sipping the same glass of anisette, with an identical smile, both fierce and complacent? Charlot worked the claw machine with automatic gestures, and there was no reason for that to stop at any given time.

The engaged couple moved the pieces on the draughts board, which they studied after every move, with unreal seriousness, while the major downed glass after glass of champagne and told stories to Mr Pyke.

No one was in a hurry. No one seemed to think that tomorrow existed. When she had no customers to serve, Jojo went and leaned on the counter with her chin on her hands, gazing thoughtfully into the distance. Several times Maigret felt her eyes focused on him, but as soon as he turned his head she was looking elsewhere.

Paul, the landlord, still wearing his chef's uniform, went from one table to the other, offering to buy a round at each. It must have cost him a lot of money, but it seemed likely that he would make it back in the end.

As for his wife, a little person with faded blonde hair and harsh features, a person you barely noticed, she sat by herself at a table and did the day's accounts.

'It's like this every evening,' Lechat had said to the chief inspector.

'And what about the people from the island, I mean the fishermen?'

'They rarely come after dinner. They go off to sea before dawn and go to bed early. In any case they wouldn't come to the Arche in the evening. It's a kind of tacit agreement. In the afternoon, or indeed the morning, everyone mixes. After dinner, the islanders, the real natives, tend to go to the other cafés.'

'What do they do?'

'Nothing. I went to see them. Sometimes they listen to the radio, but that's quite rare. They have a little glass in silence, gazing into the distance.'

'Is it always as calm here as it is now?'

'It depends. Wait. It can change from one moment to the next. It takes almost nothing, a phrase in the air, a round offered by one person or another, and everyone clusters together, and they all start talking at once.'

It hadn't happened, perhaps because of the presence of Maigret.

★

He was hot, even though the window was open. It had become a mania, listening to the sounds of the hotel. Ginette still wasn't asleep. Sometimes he heard footsteps over his head. As for Mr Pyke, he must have gone to the end of the corridor four times, and each time Maigret waited, with a kind of anxiety, for the noise of the flushing toilet before trying to go to sleep again. Because he had to go back to sleep each time it happened, and his sleep wasn't deep enough to erase his thoughts completely, just deep enough to distort them.

Mr Pyke had played a horrible trick on him by talking to him about the Dutchman as he had done at the end of the jetty. Now, the inspector could only see de Greef through the peremptory phrases of his British colleague.

But the portrait that Pyke had drawn of the young man didn't satisfy him. He was there, too, with Anna who must have been sleepy and, as time passed, fell more and more against her companion's shoulder.

De Greef didn't say a word to her. It looked as if he didn't say a word to her very often. He was the male, the boss, and she only had to wait on his every whim.

He watched. With his gaunt face he looked like a lean animal, a wild beast.

The others probably weren't lambs, but without question de Greef was a wild beast. He sniffed like a beast. It was a tic of his. He listened to all that was being said and he sniffed. It was his only perceptible reaction.

In the jungle, the major would doubtless have been a pachyderm, an elephant or, even better, a hippopotamus. And Monsieur Émile? Something furtive, with pointed teeth.

It was ridiculous. What would Mr Pyke have thought if he had been able to read Maigret's mind? It was true that the inspector had the excuse of having drunk a lot and being half asleep. If he had predicted his insomnia, he would have downed a few glasses more, to send him straight off into a dreamless slumber.

Lechat was basically a sound fellow. So sound that Maigret wished he was working for him. Still a bit young, a bit agitated. He got excited easily, like a hunting dog running in all directions around his master.

He already knew the Midi, having been part of the Draguignan brigade, but he had only had the opportunity to come to Porquerolles once or twice: he had known the island for barely three days.

'Don't the people from the *North Star* come every evening?'

'Almost every evening. Sometimes they turn up late. When the sea is calm, they often go out in the dinghy by moonlight.'

'Are Mrs Wilcox and the major friends?'

'They carefully avoid speaking to each other, and each of them looks at the other as if they could see straight through them.'

That was understandable in the end. They both belonged to the same milieu. Both, for one reason or another, came here to slum it.

The major must have been embarrassed to get drunk in front of Mrs Wilcox, because, in his country, gentlemen tend to do that among themselves, behind closed doors.

As for her, in the presence of the former officer in the Indian army, she couldn't have been proud of Moricourt.

They had arrived at about eleven o'clock in the evening. As almost always happens, she wasn't at all as the inspector had imagined her.

He had imagined an elegant English lady, and in fact she was a woman with dyed red hair, no longer in the first flush of youth, quite fat, and whose broken voice, at its most sonorous, was very like Major Bellam's. She wore a cotton dress, but she had a necklace of three rows of pearls which might have been real around her neck and a big diamond on her finger.

She had immediately looked around for Maigret. Philippe must have spoken to her about the inspector, and, once she was sitting down, she had kept on studying him and talking about him to her companion in a low voice.

What was she saying? Did she in turn find him over-weight and vulgar? Had she imagined him as a matinée idol? Perhaps she thought he didn't look very intelligent?

They were both drinking whisky, with very little soda. Philippe was very solicitous, and the inspector's attention irritated him; he clearly didn't like being seen performing his functions. As for her, she was doing it on purpose. Rather than calling Jojo or Paul, she sent her paramour to change her glass, which she did not think was clean enough, and made him get up to go and get her some cigarettes from the bar. Another time she sent him outside, God alone knew why.

She was keen to assert her power over the heir to the

Moricourt family and perhaps, at the same time, to demonstrate that she had no shame.

The couple, in passing, had greeted young de Greef and his companion. Very vaguely, the way one exchanges masonic signs.

The major, contrary to Maigret's expectations, had left first, dignified and with an uncertain step, and Mr Pyke had walked him part of the way.

Then the dentist, in his turn, had left.

'You'll see! You'll see!' he had said over and over again to Maigret, predicting that he would soon be seized by an attack of porquerollitis.

Charlot, who had had enough of the claw machine, had gone and straddled a chair beside the draughts players, silently indicating a move or two to Ginette. Once Monsieur Émile had left, he had gone upstairs to bed. Ginette seemed to be waiting for permission from Maigret. At last she had come to his table and murmured with a little smile:

'Are you still angry with me?'

She was visibly tired, and he had advised her to go up to bed. He had gone upstairs immediately after her, because it had occurred to him that she might be going to join Charlot.

Suddenly, while he was trying to go to sleep – or perhaps he was already asleep, and it was only a dream – he had had a sense of discovering a truly important fact.

'I mustn't forget it. It's indispensable for me to remember it tomorrow morning.'

He had almost got up again to jot it down on a piece

of paper. It had come to him like a flash of light. It was very curious. He was contented. He repeated to himself: 'The most important thing is not to forget it tomorrow morning!'

And the noise of the toilet flush echoed once again around the Arche. After that came another ten minutes of hearing the water running slowly into the cistern. It was exasperating. The noise got louder. There were bangs. Maigret sat up, opened his eyes and found his bedroom bathed in sunlight with, just in front of him, in the frame of the open window, the bell-tower of the little church.

The bangs were coming from the harbour. It was the engines of the boats starting up and coughing. All the fishermen were leaving at the same time. One of the engines kept stopping after firing a few times, and a silence followed, then once again that cough that you wished you could help to come out once and for all.

He wanted to get dressed and go outside, looked at the time on his watch, which he had put on his bedside table, and noted that it was only half past four in the morning. The smell was even more pronounced than it had been the previous day, probably because of the dampness of dawn. There wasn't a sound in the house, not a sound in the square, where the foliage of the eucalyptus trees had been motionless at sunrise. Only the engines in the harbour, sometimes a voice; then the hum of engines itself faded away into the distance, until, for a very long time, there was merely a vibration of the air.

When he opened his eyes again, a different smell reminded him of all the mornings since his earliest childhood, the smell of fresh coffee. Most of the rooms in the hotel were rustling, and he heard footsteps in the square, wheelbarrows squeaking on the cobblestones.

He thought immediately that he had to remember something essential, but he could find no precise memory. His mouth was sticky from the anisette. He looked for a bell-push in the hope of having coffee brought up to him. There wasn't one. Then he put on his trousers, shirt and slippers, gave his hair a quick comb and opened his door. A strong smell of perfume and soap came from Ginette's room, where she was probably washing herself.

Wasn't she the subject of the discovery he had made, or thought he had made? He went downstairs and, in the dining room, found the chairs forming pyramids on the tables. The doors were open, and the chairs from the terrace were similarly stacked. There was no one there.

He went into the kitchen, which looked dark to him, and had to accustom his eyes to the gloom.

'Good morning, inspector. Did you sleep well?'

It was Jojo, in her dress, which was too short and literally clung to her skin. She hadn't washed either and she seemed to be naked under it.

'Will you have some coffee?'

For a moment he thought of Madame Maigret, who, at this time of day, would be preparing breakfast in their Paris apartment, with the windows open on to Boulevard Richard-Lenoir. It struck him that it was probably raining in Paris. When he had left, it was almost as cold as in winter. From here, that seemed incredible.

'Do you want me to clear a table for you?'

What for? He was perfectly happy in the kitchen. She was burning some vine logs in the stove, and it smelled good. When she raised her arms he saw the little brown hairs in her armpits.

He was still trying to remember his discovery of the previous day and said some words without thinking, perhaps because he felt awkward being on his own with Jojo.

'Hasn't Monsieur Paul come down?'

'He's been at the harbour for a long time. He goes there every morning to buy his fish from the boats when they come back in.'

She glanced at the clock.

'The *Cormoran* leaves in five minutes.'

'Hasn't anyone else come down?'

'Monsieur Charlot.'

'Not with his luggage, I suppose?'

'No. He's with Monsieur Paul. Your friend left as well, at least half an hour ago.'

Maigret studied the expanse of the square through the open doors.

'He must be in the water. He was in his swimming trunks, with a towel under his arm.'

It had something to do with Ginette. But in his mind it had something to do with Jojo too. He remembered that, in his half-sleep, he had thought about Jojo climbing the stairs. And yet it wasn't an erotic thought. It was only incidentally about the glimpse of her legs. Let's see! Then she had come into his room.

The day before he had insistently asked Ginette:

'Why did you come?'

And she had lied several times. First of all she had declared that it was to see him, because she had learned that he was on the island and that she had suspected he would put out a search for her.

A little later she admitted that she was somehow engaged to Monsieur Émile. Which meant admitting that she had come to exonerate him and to tell the inspector that her boss had nothing to do with Marcellin's death.

He hadn't been so wrong to be harsh with her. She had opened up a little, just not enough.

He drank his coffee in little sips, standing by the stove. By some curious coincidence, the cup, a vulgar, vintage piece of china, was almost a perfect replica of the one he had used during his childhood and which he had considered unique at the time.

'Aren't you eating anything?'

'Not now.'

'In a quarter of an hour there will be fresh bread at the bakery.'

He relaxed at last, and Jojo must have wondered what it was that was making him smile. It had come to him. Hadn't Marcellin talked to Jojo about a 'fat packet' that he could have made? He was drunk, perhaps, but then he was often drunk. For how long had he had the chance of winning that packet? There was no guarantee that it was very recent. Ginette came to the island almost every month. She had come the previous month. It was easy to check. Marcellin, on the other hand, could have written to her.

If he had a chance of making a fat packet, it was likely

that someone else could do it in his stead, by knowing what he knew, for example.

Maigret sat there, his cup in his hand, staring at the luminous rectangle of the door, and Jojo kept glancing curiously at him.

Lechat claimed that Marcel had died because he had talked too much about 'his friend Maigret', and at first that sounded far-fetched.

It was funny to see Mr Pyke, almost naked, standing out against the light, wet towel in hand, hair glued to his forehead.

Rather than greeting him, Maigret murmured:

'Just a moment . . .'

He was nearly there. A small effort, and the ideas would fit together. Starting, for example, with the idea that Ginette had come because she knew why Marcellin had died.

She hadn't necessarily gone to any great lengths to prevent the discovery of the guilty man. Once she had married Monsieur Émile she would be rich, either way. Except that old Justine wasn't dead, she could drag on for years in spite of the doctors. If she learned what was being planned, she was quite capable of doing something stupid to prevent her son from marrying anyone after her death.

Marcellin's 'fat packet' was the issue of the moment. Might there still be a chance of someone getting hold of it? In spite of the presence of Maigret and Inspector Lechat?

'Forgive me, Mr Pyke. Did you sleep well?'

'Very well,' the Englishman replied imperturbably.

Was Maigret going to admit to him that he had counted

the times the toilet had flushed? There was no point, and after his swim in the sea the inspector from Scotland Yard was fresh as a fish.

Soon, while shaving, the inspector would have time to think about that 'fat packet'.

6. The Major's Horse

The English have their good points. Would a French colleague, in Mr Pyke's place, have resisted the urge to score a point? And hadn't Maigret, who wasn't particularly inclined to tease, nearly made a discreet allusion, just now, to the toilet flush that the inspector from Scotland Yard had pulled so often during the night?

Perhaps the drink had flown more freely the previous evening than either of them had noticed. At any rate, it was quite unexpected. All three of them, Maigret, Pyke and Jojo, were still in the kitchen, whose door was still open. Maigret was finishing his coffee, and Mr Pyke, in his swimming costume, interposed himself between Maigret and the light, while Jojo tried to find him some bacon in the larder. It was exactly three minutes to eight and then, looking at the clock, Maigret announced in one of those innocent, inimitable voices that come to you as you are making a gaffe:

'I wonder if Lechat is still sleeping off last night's tipples.'

Jojo gave a start, but was careful not to turn round. As to Mr Pyke, all his good manners could not prevent what looked like spots of astonishment appearing all over his face. But it was with perfect simplicity that he articulated:

'I've just learned what was happening on board the *Cormoran*. I expect he'll be waiting for Ginette.'

Maigret had completely forgotten about Marcellin's funeral. Even worse, it suddenly came back to him that the previous day he had been talking about it at length, perhaps even too insistently, to his colleague. Had Mr Pyke been in on that conversation? He couldn't have said, but he saw himself again, sitting on the banquette.

'You go with her, my friend, you understand? I'm not claiming it will get us anywhere. Perhaps she will react, perhaps she won't. Perhaps someone will try to speak to her on the sly? Perhaps if she recognizes a face among the mourners it might tell you something? You always have to go to funerals, it's an old principle that has often paid off for me. Keep your eyes open. That's all.'

He even thought he remembered, as he addressed the inspector with the familiar *tu*, that he had told him two or three stories about funerals that had put him on the trail of criminals.

Now he understood why Ginette had been making so much noise in her room. He heard her opening her door and calling out from upstairs:

'Bring me a cup of coffee quickly, Jojo. How long have I got?'

'Three minutes!'

At that very moment a toot from the *Cormoran*'s whistle announced its imminent departure.

'I'll go to the landing stage,' Maigret announced.

In slippers and without his false collar, because he hadn't had time to go upstairs and get dressed. He wasn't the only one in a similar outfit. There were little clusters of people near the boat, the very same ones who had been there the previous day when Maigret had disembarked. They must have been there for all departures and arrivals. Before they began their day, they came to look at the *Cormoran* leaving the harbour, after which, putting off their morning wash a little longer, they had a glass of white wine at Paul's bar or in one of the cafés.

The dentist, less discreet than Mr Pyke, stared pointedly at Maigret's slippers and untidy appearance, and his smug smile said unambiguously:

'I told you! It's starting!'

Porquerollitis, clearly, which had infected him to the bone. Out loud, he merely asked:

'Sleep well?'

Lechat, already on board, petulant and impatient, got back off the boat to talk to Maigret.

'I didn't want to wake you. Isn't she coming? Baptiste says that if she doesn't come straight away they'll leave without her.'

Other people were crossing the water to go to Marcellin's funeral, fishermen in their Sunday best, the bricklayer, the tobacconist. Maigret couldn't see Charlot anywhere around, even though he had spotted him in the square shortly before. Nothing stirred on board the *North Star*. Just as the mute was about to light anchor, Ginette appeared, half walking, half running, dressed in black silk, with a black hat and a little veil, leaving a rustling, perfumed wake. They hoisted her on board as if in a conjuring trick, and it was only once she was sitting down that she saw the inspector on the quay and gave a little nod of greeting.

The sea was so smooth and so bright that, when you stared at it for a long time, for a moment it was impossible to make out the outlines of objects. The *Cormoran* drew a silvery curve on the water. The people stood and watched after it for a moment, out of habit and tradition, before setting off slowly towards the square. A fisherman, who had just speared an octopus with his trident, was skinning it as its tentacles rolled around his tattooed arm.

At the Arche, Paul, clear-eyed, was serving white wine behind his bar, and Mr Pyke, who had had time to get dressed, was eating bacon and eggs at a table. Maigret had a glass, like the others, and a little later, when he was shaving at his window, braces dangling at his thighs, there was a knock at his door.

It was the Englishman.

'I hope I'm not disturbing you. May I come in?'

He sat down on the only chair, and there was quite a long silence.

'I spent part of the evening chatting with the major,' he said at last. 'Did you know he was one of our most famous polo players?'

He must have been disappointed by Maigret's reaction, or rather his lack of reaction. He only had a vague idea about the game of polo. At most he knew it was played on horseback, and that somewhere, in the Bois de Boulogne or Saint-Cloud, there was a very aristocratic polo club.

Mr Pyke casually threw him a line.

'He's the youngest son.'

That must have meant a lot to him. Isn't it true that in England, in the grand families, the eldest alone inherits the title and the fortune, forcing the others to forge a career in the army or the navy?

'His brother is in the House of Lords. The major chose the Indian army.'

The same phenomenon must have happened in reverse when Maigret talked in passing to his English colleague about people like Charlot, like Monsieur Émile, like Ginette. But Mr Pyke was patient, he dotted the 'i's with exquisite discretion and impeccable delicacy.

'When you have a certain name, you are reluctant to stay in London if you can't afford to cut a figure there. Horses are the great passion in the Indian army. To play polo you need a stable of several ponies.'

'Did the major never marry?'

'Youngest sons seldom do. If he had taken on the responsibility of a family, Bellam would have had to give up the horses.'

'And he preferred the horses!'

That didn't seem to surprise Mr Pyke in the slightest.

'In the evening, over there, bachelors meet at the club, and drinking is their only distraction. The major has done a lot of drinking in his life. In India, it was whisky. It's only here that he's started on the champagne.'

'Did he tell you why he has chosen to live in Porquer-olles?'

'There was a terrible disaster, the worst that could have happened to him. Following a bad fall from a horse, he was bedridden for three years, half of that time in plaster, and once he was back on his feet, he knew that horse-riding was now out of the question for him.'

'Is that why he left India?'

'It's why he's here. I'm sure that in climates like this one, in the Mediterranean or the Pacific, you would find plenty of old gentlemen like the major who are seen as eccentrics. Where else could they go?'

'Don't they want to go back to England?'

'Their resources wouldn't allow them to live in London according to their rank, and the habits they have assumed would be frowned upon in the English countryside.'

'Did he tell you why he won't say hello to Mrs Wilcox?'

'He didn't need to.'

Did he have to press the matter? Or would Mr Pyke have preferred not to hear too much about his compatriot? But in the end Mrs Wilcox was the major's female equivalent.

Maigret wiped his cheeks and hesitated to put on his jacket. The inspector from the Yard hadn't put his on. It was already hot. But unlike his slim colleague the inspector couldn't afford not to wear braces, and a man in braces always looks like a shopkeeper on a picnic.

He put on his jacket. They had nothing further to do in the room, where Mr Pyke, as he rose to his feet, murmured:

'The major, in spite of everything, is still a gentleman.'

He followed Maigret to the stairs. He didn't ask him what he planned to do but he followed him, and that was enough to spoil the inspector's day.

He had vaguely promised himself, precisely because of Mr Pyke, to behave as a senior police officer that morning. In principle, a detective chief inspector in the

Police Judiciaire doesn't walk the streets and hang out in bars in search of a murderer. He is an important gentleman, who spends most of his time in his office and, from his headquarters, like a general, directs a little army of sergeants, inspectors and technicians.

Maigret had never been able to resign himself to that. Like a hunting dog, he needed to go ferreting things out in person, scratching and sniffing for scents.

For the first two days, Lechat had done a considerable amount of work and had given Maigret an account of all the interrogations in which he had been involved. The whole island had been questioned, the Morins and the Gallis, the sick doctor, the priest, whom Maigret hadn't yet seen, and the women as well.

So Maigret had to sit in a corner of the dining room, which was deserted all morning, and seriously study the reports, marking them with a blue or red pencil.

With an anxious little glance, he asked Mr Pyke:

'Do your colleagues at the Yard sometimes walk the streets like rookies?'

'I know at least three or four that you never see in their offices.'

All the better, because he wanted to get back on his feet. He was beginning to understand why you always met the people of Porquerolles in the same places. It was instinctive. In some way, in spite of themselves, they had been swallowed up by the sun, by the landscape. Now, for example, Maigret and his companion were taking an aimless little stroll outside and barely noticed that they were walking down towards the harbour.

Maigret was sure that, if for any reason he had to spend the rest of his days on the island, he would take the same walk every morning, and that the pipe he smoked when he did so would always be the best pipe of the day. The *Cormoran*, down there, on the other side of the water, at the Giens headland, was disembarking its passengers, who were boarding an old bus. Even with the naked eye the boat could be seen as a tiny white dot.

The mute would load the cases of fruit and vegetables for the mayor, for the Cooperative, meat for the butcher, the mail sacks. People would embark, just as Maigret and Mr Pyke had done the day before, and would doubtless be dazzled as the two men had been at the sight of the underwater landscape.

The sailors on the big white yacht were polishing the deck. They were middle-aged men who went for a tipple from time to time, without mingling with the locals, at Morin-Barbu's.

On the right of the harbour, a path climbed the steep, rugged slope, leading to a shack with an open door.

A fisherman, sitting in the doorway, held a net stretched out with his toes, and his hands, deft as a seamstress's, were passing a shuttle through the meshes.

It was there that Marcellin had been killed. The two policemen glanced inside. The centre was occupied by a huge cauldron like the ones used in the countryside for boiling up pig-fodder. Here it was the nets that were set to boil, in a brown mixture which protected them against the seawater.

Marcellin's mattress must have been made of old sails,

and lying around in the corners were pots of paint, cans of oil or petrol, scrap metal and patched-up oars.

'Do other people sleep here?' Maigret asked the fisherman.

He lifted his head indifferently.

'Old Benoît, sometimes, when it's raining.'

'And when it's not?'

'Then he'd rather sleep outside. It depends. Sometimes in a rocky inlet or on the deck of a ship. And sometimes on a bench in the square.'

'Have you seen him today?'

'He was over there just now.'

The fisherman pointed to the path that ran along the sea at a considerable height and was lined with pine trees on one side.

'Was he alone?'

'I think the gentleman who's at the Arche joined him a bit further on.'

'Which one?'

'The one who wears a cotton suit and a white cap.'

It was Charlot.

'Did he come back this way?'

'About half an hour ago.'

The *Cormoran* was only a white dot in the blue of the world, but that white dot had now clearly detached itself from the shore. Other boats were scattered across the sea, some of them motionless, some drifting slowly, pulling a luminous wake behind them.

Maigret and Mr Pyke walked back down towards the

harbour and along the jetty, as they had done the previous evening, and mechanically watched a little boy fishing for conger eel with a short line.

When they passed in front of the Dutchman's little boat, Maigret glanced inside and was rather surprised to see Charlot in conversation with de Greef.

Mr Pyke continued on in silence. Was he waiting for something to happen? Was he trying to guess Maigret's thoughts?

They walked to the end of the jetty, retraced their steps, passed once more in front of the *Fleur d'amour*, and Charlot was still in the same place.

Three times they walked the hundred metres of the jetty, and the third time Charlot climbed on to the deck of the little yacht, turned to say goodbye and stepped on to the gangplank.

The two men were very close to him. Their paths were about to cross. Maigret hesitated for a moment and then stopped. It was the time of day when the bus from Giens was supposed to arrive in Hyères. The people from the funeral would go for a drink before going to the morgue.

'Tell me, I was looking for you this morning.'

'As you can see, I haven't left the island.'

'That's exactly what I want to talk to you about. I can't see any reason to keep you here. You told me, I think, that you'd only come for two or three days, and that if Marcellin hadn't died you would have left again already. The inspector thought it was a good idea to keep you here. I am granting you your freedom.'

'Thank you.'

'I would just ask you to tell me where I can find you if I need you.'

Charlot, who was smoking a cigarette, looked thoughtfully at its tip for a moment.

'At the Arche!' he said at last.

'You're not leaving?'

'Not for the moment.'

And, raising his head, he stared into the inspector's eyes.

'Are you surprised? It almost looks as if you're annoyed to see me staying. I assume I'm allowed to.'

'I can't stop you. I confess that I would be curious to know what made you change your mind.'

'I don't have a particularly absorbing profession, do I? No office, no factory, no business, no employees or workmen waiting for me. Don't you think it's nice here?'

He made no attempt to conceal his irony. The mayor, still in a long grey overall, could be seen going down towards the harbour, pushing a handcart. The tout for the Grand Hôtel was there too, and the postman with his official cap.

The *Cormoran* was now right in the middle of the channel and would reach the landing stage in a quarter of an hour.

'Did you have a long conversation with old Benoît?'

'When I spotted you near the shack just now, I thought you'd ask that. You'll question Benoît in turn, I can't stop you, but I can tell you in advance that he doesn't know anything. At least that's what I thought I understood, because it isn't easy to interpret his language. Perhaps after all you'll have more luck than I did.'

'Are you looking for something?'

'Perhaps the same thing as you.'

It was almost a challenge, delivered with good humour.

'What makes you think that he might be of interest? Did Marcellin talk to you?'

'No more than to anyone else. He was always a bit awkward with me. The small fry aren't at ease with the big shots.'

In a while he would have to explain the slang to Mr Pyke, who was clearly putting it in a box in his brain.

Maigret joined in, he too talking casually, in a light tone, as if saying nothing of any importance.

'Do you know why Marcellin was killed, Charlot?'

'I know about as much as you, and God knows, I probably draw the same conclusions as you do, but to other ends.'

He smiled and squinted into the sun.

'Has Jojo talked to you?'

'To me? Haven't they told you that we hate each other like a cat and a dog?'

'Did you do something to her?'

'She wasn't interested. That's exactly what keeps us apart.'

'I wonder, Charlot, if you wouldn't be better off going back to Pont du Las.'

'Thanks for your advice, but I'd rather stay here.'

A dinghy detached itself from the *North Star*, and on

board the silhouette of Moricourt could be made out taking the oars. He was alone on the boat. Probably, like the others, he was coming to meet the *Cormoran* and would go up to the post office to get his mail.

Charlot, who was watching Maigret's eyes, seemed at the same time to be following his thoughts. As the inspector was turned towards the Dutchman's boat, he said:

'He's a strange young man, but I don't think he did it.'

'Do you mean Marcellin's murder?'

'There's no hiding anything from you. Bear in mind that I'm not interested in the murderer in himself. Only in the course of an argument you don't kill someone for no reason, do you? Even if, and especially if, he tells anyone who will listen that he's a friend of Detective Chief Inspector Maigret.'

'Were you at the Arche when Marcellin talked about me?'

'Everyone was there, I mean everyone you're interested in right now. And Marcellin had quite a piercing voice, particularly when he'd had a drop or two.'

'Do you know why he said that, on that particular evening?'

'And there you are. It's the first question I asked myself when I found out he was dead. I wondered who the poor guy was talking to. You understand?'

Maigret understood perfectly.

'Have you found a satisfactory answer?'

'Not yet. If I had, I'd head back to Pont du Las on the next boat.'

'I didn't know you liked playing amateur detectives.'

'You're joking, inspector.'

Maigret was still trying, without seeming to do so, to make his partner say something that he was refusing to say.

It was an odd game, in the sun by the jetty, with Mr Pyke playing the part of referee and remaining scrupulously neutral.

'So you're definitely starting from the assumption that Marcellin wasn't killed for no reason.'

'As you say.'

'You're assuming that his murderer was trying to get hold of something that Marcellin had in his possession.'

'Neither of us is assuming any such thing, or else your reputation is vastly overrated.'

'They wanted to silence him?'

'You're getting warm, inspector.'

'He'd discovered something that put someone in danger?'

'Why are you so keen to know what I think, when you know as much as I do?'

'Even about the "fat packet"?'

'Even about the "fat packet".'

After which, Charlot, lighting a new cigarette, said:

'I've always been interested in that, do you get it now?'

'Is that why you visited the Dutchman this morning?'

'He hasn't got two pennies to rub together.'

'Which means it wasn't him?'

'I didn't say that. I'm just saying that Marcellin couldn't have hoped to get any money out of him.'

'You're forgetting the girl.'

'Anna?'

'Her father is very rich.'

That made Charlot think for a moment, but in the end he just shrugged his shoulders. The *Cormoran* was passing the first rocky headland and coming into the harbour.

'Will you excuse me? I may be expecting someone.'

And Charlot ironically touched his cap and headed towards the landing stage.

While Maigret stuffed his pipe, Mr Pyke said:

'I think that chap is very intelligent.'

'It's quite difficult to succeed in his trade if you're not.'

The tout for the Grand Hôtel was taking charge of the luggage of a young married couple. The mayor, who had come on board, was checking the labels on the parcels. Charlot helped a young woman to step down and led her towards the Arche. So he really was waiting for someone. He must have phoned the day before.

Come to think of it, where had Inspector Lechat telephoned Maigret from two evenings earlier to tell him what had happened? If it was from the Arche, the phone on the wall was close to the bar, which meant that everyone had heard him. He would have to think about asking him about that.

The dentist was there again, wearing the same clothes as he had that morning, unshaven, perhaps unwashed, with an old straw hat on his head. He was watching the *Cormoran*, and that was enough for him. He seemed happy to be alive.

Were Maigret and Mr Pyke going to follow the general movement, climb slowly up to the Arche, approach the bar and drink the white wine they would be served without being asked what they would like?

Maigret studied his companion out of the corner of his eye, and in turn Mr Pyke, although impassive, looked as if he was spying on him.

Why do anything differently from the others, after all? Marcellin's funeral was happening in Hyères. Behind the hearse, Ginette was standing in for family, and she would be dabbing her face with her handkerchief rolled in a ball. It would be sultry over there, in the avenues lined with motionless palm trees.

'Do you like the white wine from the island, Mr Pyke?'

'It's very drinkable.'

The postman was crossing the bare expanse of the square, pushing a cart with the mail sacks heaped up on it. Raising his head, Maigret saw the windows of the Arche wide open, and framed in one of them Charlot, on the first floor, leaning on the railing. Behind him, in the gilded gloom, a young woman was taking off her dress, pulling it over her head.

'He's talked a lot, and I wonder if he didn't want to tell me more.'

That would come later. People like Charlot find it hard to resist the desire to gain the upper hand. While Maigret and Mr Pyke were sitting down on the terrace, they saw Monsieur Émile, more of a little white mouse than ever, on the square, walking with tiny steps, a panama hat on his head, crossing diagonally towards the post office, to the left of the church, right at the end. The door was open.

Four or five people were waiting while the postmistress sorted the mail.

It was Saturday. Jojo was washing the red tiles of the bar with lots of water. Her feet were bare, and streams of water dripped on to the terrace.

Paul brought not two glasses of white wine, but a bottle.

'Do you know the woman who's gone up to Charlot's room?'

'She's his girlfriend.'

'Is she a working girl?'

'I don't think so. She's some sort of dancer or singer in a nightclub in Marseille. It's the third or fourth time she's come here.'

'Did he telephone her?'

'Yesterday afternoon, while you were in your room.'

'Do you know what he said?'

'He just asked her to come and spend the weekend. She accepted straight away.'

'Were Charlot and Marcellin friends?'

'I don't remember ever seeing them together, I mean just the two of them.'

'I'd like you to try to remember exactly. When Marcellin talked about me in the evening . . .'

'I understand what you mean. Your colleague asked me the same question.'

'I suppose that at the start of the evening the customers were sitting at different tables, like yesterday evening?'

'Yes. It always starts that way.'

'Do you know what happened then?'

'Someone put on the record player, I can't remember

who. But I remember that there was music. The Dutch-man and his girlfriend started dancing. I remember that because I noticed that she let him throw her around in his arms like a rag doll.'

'Did anyone else dance?'

'Mrs Wilcox and Monsieur Philippe. He's a very good dancer.'

'Where was Marcellin when this was happening?'

'I think I can see him at the bar.'

'Very drunk?'

'Not very, but quite . . . Wait. One detail. He insisted on having a dance with Mrs Wilcox . . .'

'Marcellin?'

Was it deliberate that when he spoke of his compatriot Mr Pyke suddenly appeared lost in thought?

'Did she accept?'

'They took a few steps. Marcellin must have stumbled. He liked acting the clown when there were people around. He was the one who paid for the first round. That's right. There was a bottle of whisky on their table. She doesn't like it being served by the glass. Marcellin drank some and asked for white wine.'

'The major?'

'I was just thinking about him. He was in the opposite corner, and I'm trying to think who he had with him. I think it was Polyte.'

'Who's Polyte?'

'A Morin. The one with the green boat. In the summer he organizes the tour of the island for the tourists. He wears a long-haul captain's cap.'

'Is he a captain?'

'He served in the navy and must hold the rank of quartermaster. He often went to Toulon with the major. The dentist drank with them. Marcellin started going from one table to the other, with his glass, and if I'm not mistaken he mixed his white wine with whisky.'

'How did he start talking about me? Who was he talking to? Was he at the major's table or Mrs Wilcox's?'

'I'm doing my best. You've seen how it works, and yesterday evening was a calm one. The Dutch couple were close to Mrs Wilcox. I think it was at that table that the conversation began. Marcellin was standing in the middle of the room, when I heard him exclaim, 'My friend, Detective Chief Inspector Maigret . . . My very good friend, and I know what I'm saying . . . I can prove it . . .'

'Did he show them a letter?'

'Not to my knowledge. I was busy, with Jojo, serving.'

'Was your wife in the bar?'

'I think she'd gone upstairs. She usually goes upstairs when she's finished the accounts. She isn't very well and she needs a lot of sleep.'

'So Marcellin might equally well have been talking to Major Bellam and Mrs Wilcox as to the Dutchman? Or even to Charlot or someone else? To the dentist, for example? To Monsieur Émile?'

'I think so.'

He was wanted inside and left them with an apology. The people coming out of the post office were starting to cross the sunlit expanse of the square, where, in a corner, a woman was standing behind a table on which she had arranged a display of vegetables. Beside the Arche the mayor was unloading crates.

'You're wanted on the telephone, Monsieur Maigret.'

He entered the gloom of the café and picked up the receiver.

'Is that you, chief? Lechat here. It's over. I'm in a bar near the cemetery. The lady you know is with me. She hasn't left my side since the *Cormoran*. She has had time to tell me her life story.'

'How did it go?'

'Very well. She bought some flowers. Other islanders left some at the grave. It was very hot at the cemetery. I don't know what to decide. I think I'm going to be obliged to invite her to lunch.'

'Can she hear you?'

'No. I'm in a cabin. I can see her in the window. She's putting on some powder and looking at herself in a little mirror.'

'And has she met anyone? Has she made a phone call?'

'She hasn't left me for a second. I even had to go with her to the florist's and, behind the hearse, since I was walking beside her, I looked like I was part of the family.'

'Did you take the bus to go from Giens to Hyères?'

'I couldn't help but invite her to get into my car. Is everything all right on the island?'

'Everything's fine.'

When he came back on to the terrace, Maigret found the dentist sitting beside Mr Pyke and clearly waiting to share the bottle of white wine.

Philippe de Moricourt, with a stack of newspapers under his arm, was hovering on the doorstep of the Arche.

Monsieur Émile walked cautiously towards his villa, where old Justine was waiting for him, and, as always, from the kitchen there came the smell of bouillabaisse.

7. The Postmistress's Afternoon

It wasn't a nickname. The fat girl hadn't chosen it herself. She really had been christened Aglaé. She was very fat, particularly from the waist down, misshapen like a woman of fifty or sixty who's grown fat with age, and by contrast her face only looked all the more childish, because Aglaé couldn't have been more than twenty-six.

That afternoon Maigret had discovered a whole new district of Porquerolles when, still accompanied by Mr Pyke, he had crossed to the other side of the square for the first time to go to the post office. Was that really the scent of incense emanating from the little church, where solemn mass must have been a rare event?

It was the same square as the one facing the Arche, and yet you would have sworn that the air at the top end was hotter and thicker. The little gardens in front of two or three houses were jumbles of flowers and bees. The sounds coming from the harbour were very faint. Two old men were playing a version of boules where they didn't throw the balls more than a few metres from their feet, and it was curious to see them carefully bending down.

One of them was Ferdinand Galli, the patriarch of all the Gallis on the island, who kept a café in the corner of the square, a café that the inspector had never seen anyone go up to. It must have been frequented only by neighbours, or by the Gallis of the tribe. His companion was a neat and tidy pensioner who was entirely deaf, who wore a railwayman's cap; another octogenarian, sitting on the post office bench, looked at them as he dozed.

Because beside the open door of the post office there was a green painted bench, on which Maigret was going to spend part of his afternoon.

'I was wondering if you would eventually find your way up here!' Aglaé had exclaimed when she saw him come in. 'I suspected that you would need to make a phone call, and you wouldn't be too pleased about doing it at the Arche, where so many people can hear what you're saying.'

'Will it take a long time to get through to Paris?'

'As a priority call, I'll have it for you in a few minutes.'

'Then ask for the Police Judiciaire.'

'I know the number. I was the one who connected you when your inspector called you.'

He almost asked her:

'And did you listen?'

But she would soon inform him all by herself.

'Who do you want to speak to, at the Police Judiciaire?'

'Sergeant Lucas. If he isn't there, Inspector Torrence.'

A few moments later, he had Lucas on the line.

'What's the weather like up there, old man? It's still raining? Showers? Good! Listen, Lucas. Sort me out with some information about someone called Philippe de Moricourt. Yes. Lechat has seen his papers and claims it's his real name. His last address in Paris was a furnished flat on the Left Bank, Rue Jacob, at 17 bis . . . What I want to know exactly? I have no preconceived idea. Anything you can find out. I don't think he has a file in Records, but you can always check. Do as much as you can by phone and then call me here. No number. Just Porquerolles. I'd also like you to call the police in Ostende. Ask if they know someone called Bebelmans, who is, I think, an important ship-owner. Same thing. Anything you can find. That's not all. Don't cut me off, mademoiselle. Do you have any acquaintances in Montparnasse? See what anyone has to say about one Jef de Greef, a sort of painter who lived on the Seine for a while, on his boat moored near the Pont-Marie. Have you taken note of that? That's all, yes. Don't wait to have all the information before calling me back. Put as many people as you like on it. Everything all right, at the office . . .? Who's had a baby . . .? Janvier's wife . . .? Congratulations from me.'

When he left the cabin he saw Aglaé, calmly and without a hint of embarrassment, taking her headset off.

'Do you always listen in to conversations?'

'I stayed on the line in case you were cut off. I don't trust the operator in Hyères, who is a bit of a minx.'

'Do you do the same for everyone?'

'I have no time in the morning because of the mail, but in the afternoon it's easier.'

'Do you keep a record of the calls requested by the people who live on the island?'

'I have to.'

'Could you draw me up a list of all the calls you've put through over the last few days? Let's say the last week.'

'Straight away. I'll have it for you in a few minutes.'

'And you're also the one who receives telegrams, is that right?'

'There aren't many, except during the season. I had one this morning that's bound to interest you.'

'How do you know?'

'It's a telegram that someone sent here, someone who looks as if he's interested in at least one of the people you've come to ask for information about.'

'Do you have a copy?'

'I'll find it for you.'

A moment later she was holding out a form to the inspector, who read:

Fred Masson, chez Angelo, Rue Blanche, Paris.
Request complete information on Philippe de Moricourt
address Rue Jacob Paris *stop* Please telegram Porquerolles.
Best.
Signed: Charlot.

Maigret showed it to Mr Pyke, who merely shook his head.

'Will you prepare me that list of calls? I'll wait outside with my friend.'

So, for the first time, they went and sat down on the bench, in the shadow of the eucalyptus trees in the square, and the wall behind them was pink and hot. Somewhere out of sight there was a fig tree, whose sweet smell they inhaled.

'In a short while,' said Mr Pyke, looking at the church clock, 'I will ask your permission to leave you temporarily, if you don't mind.'

Was it out of politeness that he pretended to think that Maigret would be sorry?

'The major has invited me to have a drink in his villa at about five o'clock. I would have hurt him if I'd refused.'

'Be my guest.'

'I thought you would probably be busy.'

After a pause just long enough for the inspector to smoke a pipe, while watching the two old men playing boules, Aglaé called in a shrill voice through her window: 'Monsieur Maigret! It's ready!'

He went and got the piece of paper she was holding out to him and came back to sit down next to the man from the Yard.

She had done her work conscientiously, with a school-girl's careful handwriting, and with three or four spelling mistakes.

The word 'butcher' appeared on the list several times. Apparently he called Hyères every day to order the next day's meat. Then there was the Cooperative, whose calls were just as frequent but more varied.

Maigret drew a line a little way below the middle of the list, separating the calls that had been made before Marcellin's death and the ones made after it.

'Are you taking notes?' Mr Pyke observed, seeing his companion opening a big notebook.

Didn't that imply that for the first time he was seeing Maigret behaving like a real detective chief inspector?

The name that appeared most often on the list was Justine's. She called Nice, Marseille, Béziers and Avignon, and, a week before, there had been four calls to Paris.

'We'll see that in a little while,' Maigret said. 'I assume the postmistress was careful to listen. Do they do that in England as well?'

'I don't think it's legal, but it may happen on occasion.'

The day before, Charlot had called Marseille. Maigret already knew. It was to bring his girlfriend, the one seen disembarking from the *Cormoran*, with whom he was now playing cards on the terrace of the Arche.

Because they could see the Arche some way off, with silhouettes moving around it. From here, where it was so calm, it looked as busy as a beehive.

The most interesting thing was that the name of Marcellin was on the list. He had called a number in Nice, exactly two days before he died.

All of a sudden Maigret went into the post office, and Mr Pyke followed him.

'Do you know what this number is, mademoiselle?'

'Of course. It's the house where the lady works. Justine asks for it every day: you can see it on the list.'

'Have you listened to Justine's conversations?'

'Often, I don't bother any more, because it's always the same thing.'

'Does she do the talking, or her son?'

'She talks, and Monsieur Émile listens.'

'I don't understand.'

'She's deaf. So Monsieur Émile puts the receiver to his ear, and he repeats what they say to her. Then she shouts so loudly into the phone that you can hardly make out the syllables. Her first words are always: how much? They give her the figures for the takings. Monsieur Émile, beside her, takes written notes. She calls each of her houses in turn.'

'I assume that it's Ginette who answers in Nice?'

'Yes, because she's the madam's assistant.'

'And the calls to Paris?'

'There aren't as many of those. Always to the same person, one Monsieur Louis. And always to ask about women. He tells her the age and price. She answers yes or no. She sometimes haggles as if she was at a village fair.'

'You didn't notice anything particular in her conversations recently? Monsieur Émile didn't call in person?'

'I don't think he would dare.'

'His mother won't let him?'

'She hardly lets him do anything.'

'And Marcellin?'

'I was going to talk to you about that. He rarely came to the office, and then it was only to pick up his cheques. I don't think he's made three phone calls in a year.'

'Who to?'

'Once it was to Toulon, to order a part for an engine that he needed for his boat. Another time to Nice . . .'

'To Ginette?'

'It was to tell her that he hadn't been able to cash the cheque. He received a cheque almost every month, you know? She had made a mistake. The sum in letters wasn't the same as the sum in figures, and I couldn't pay it. She sent another one by the next post.'

'How long ago was that?'

'About three months. The door was closed, which means that it was cold, so it was in the winter.'

'And the last call?'

'I started listening, as usual, but Madame Galli came in to buy some stamps.'

'Was it a long conversation?'

'Longer than usual. It's easy to check.'

She flicked through her book.

'Two three-minute units.'

'You heard the beginning . . . What did Marcellin say?'

'More or less this: "Is that you . . .? It's me . . . yes. No, he didn't have any money . . . I could have as much money as I wanted . . ."'

'She didn't say anything?'

'She murmured, "You've been drinking again, Marcel."'

'He swore he'd hardly touched a drop. He went on: "I'd like you to do me a favour . . . Is there a big Larousse encyclopedia in the house?" That's all I know. At that moment Madame Galli came in, and she's not an easy woman to deal with. She makes out it's her taxes that pay our wages and she's always talking about lodging a complaint.'

'Because the communication only lasted six minutes, it's unlikely that Ginette had the time to go and consult the Larousse, come back to the phone and give Marcellin an answer.'

'She sent her answer by telegram. Here! I've prepared it for you.'

She held out a yellow form, on which he read:

Died in 1890.

It was signed: Ginette.

'It would have been your bad luck if you hadn't come up to see me, wouldn't it? I wouldn't have gone down, and you'd have been none the wiser.'

'Did you see Marcellin's face when he read that telegram?'

'He reread it two or three times, to check that it was genuine, then he went out, whistling.'

'As if he'd received some good news?'

'Exactly. And also, I think, as if he was suddenly filled with admiration for someone.'

'Did you listen to Charlot's conversation yesterday?'

'With Bébé?'

'What do you mean?'

'He calls her Bébé. She must have arrived this morning. Do you want me to repeat his words? He said: "How are you, Bébé?" "Can't complain, thanks." "I've got another few days here and I'm ready to play. So come."'

'And she came,' Maigret concluded. 'Thank you, mademoiselle. I'll be outside on the bench with a friend, waiting for a call from Paris.'

Three-quarters of an hour passed as he watched the game of boules; the young married couple came to send postcards; the butcher came in turn to ask for his daily communication with Hyères. Mr Pyke looked at the church bell-tower from time to time. He sometimes opened his mouth as well, perhaps to ask a question, but every time he changed his mind.

They were both filled with an agreeable warmth. In the distance they could see the men gathering for the big game of boules, the one which brings together about ten players and is played across the whole of the square until drinks or dinner time.

The dentist was part of it. The *Cormoran* had left the island for the Giens headland, from where it would bring back Inspector Lechat and Ginette.

At last Aglaé's voice called him from inside.

'Paris!' she announced.

It was Lucas, who must have taken over the inspector's office, as he usually did during Maigret's absences. Through the window, Lucas saw the Seine and the Pont Saint-Michel, while Maigret vaguely looked at Aglaé.

'I have some of the information, chief. I'm waiting for the rest from Ostend very shortly. Who should I start with?'

'Whoever you like.'

'So, this guy Moricourt. That wasn't difficult. Torrence remembered the name from seeing it on the cover of a book. It is his real name. His father, who was a cavalry captain, died a long time ago. His mother lives in Saumur. As far as I can tell, they have no money. Several times, Philippe de Moricourt tried to marry heiresses, but it didn't work out.'

Aglaé listened brazenly and, through the glass, glanced at Maigret to emphasize the passages she liked.

'He presents himself as a man of letters. He has published two volumes of poems with a publisher on the Left Bank. He went to the Café de Flore, where he was quite well known. He also collaborated occasionally on several newspapers. What do you want to know?'

'Go on.'

'I have hardly any other details. I did all that by telephone, to gain some time; but I've sent someone to make inquiries, and you'll have some new leads this evening or tomorrow. He's never had any complaints brought against him, or more precisely there was one, five years ago, but it was dropped.'

'I'm listening.'

'A lady who lives in Auteuil, and whose name I should be given shortly, gave him a rare edition to resell, and then waited for months without hearing a word from him. She made a complaint. It was learned that he had sold the book on to an American. As for the money, he promised to give it to her in monthly instalments. I've had the former owner on the phone. Moricourt was usually two or three months late, but he did complete his payments in the end.'

'Is that all?'

'More or less. You know the type. Always well dressed, always impeccably correct.'

'And with the ladies?'

'Nothing precise. There were relationships that he was very mysterious about.'

'The other one?'

'Were you aware that they knew each other? Apparently de Greef has real merit; some people even claim that if he wanted to be, he would be one of the best painters of his generation.'

'And he doesn't want that?'

'He ends up arguing with everyone. He's run off with a Belgian girl of very good family.'

'I know.'

'Fine. When he arrived in Paris he had an exhibition of his works in a little gallery on Rue de Seine. On the last day, as he hadn't sold anything, he burned all his canvases. Some people claim that there have been real orgies on his boat. He illustrated several erotic books that are sold on the sly. That's mostly what he's lived off. And there you are, chief. I'm waiting for a call from Ostend. Is everything all right down there?'

Through the glass, Mr Pyke showed his watch to Maigret, and, as it was five o'clock, he left in the direction of the major's villa.

The inspector felt quite perky, and as if filled with a wave of holiday spirit.

'Did you pass on my congratulations to Janvier? Phone my wife and ask her to go and see his, and tell her to bring something, a present or some flowers. But not a silver christening cup!'

He found himself with Aglaé again, separated from her by the grilled partition. She seemed to be highly amused. She admitted shamelessly:

'I'd be curious to see one of his books. Do you think he has any on board?'

Then, without transition:

'It's funny! Your job is much easier than people think. Information comes from all directions. Do you think it's one of those two?'

There was a big bouquet of mimosas on her desk and a bag of sweets, which she held out to the inspector:

'Things happen here so rarely! As regards Monsieur

Philippe, I didn't think of telling you that he writes a lot. I don't read his letters, obviously. He puts them in the box, and I recognize his handwriting and his ink, because he always uses green ink, I don't know why.'

'Who does he write to?'

'I've forgotten the names, but it's almost always to Paris. From time to time he writes to his mother. The letters for Paris are much thicker.'

'Does he receive a lot of mail in return?'

'A fair amount. And magazines and newspapers. Printed matter arrives for him every day.'

'Mrs Wilcox?'

'She writes a lot as well, to England, to Capri, to Egypt. I particularly remember Egypt, because I took the liberty of asking her for stamps for my nephew.'

'Does she make phone calls?'

'Two or three times she's come to make calls from the cabin, and every time it was London that she called. Unfortunately I don't understand English.'

She added:

'I'm going to close now. I should have closed at five o'clock. But if you'd like to stay and wait for your call . . .'

'What call?'

'Didn't Monsieur Lucas tell you he was going to call you about Ostend?'

She probably wasn't dangerous, but Maigret preferred, if only for the locals, not to spend too much time chatting to her. She was filled with curiosity. She asked him, for example:

'Aren't you going to phone your wife?'

He told her he would be in the square, not far from the Arche, just in case someone called him, and he went calmly down, smoking his pipe, towards the big game of boules. He didn't have to be on his best behaviour, because Mr Pyke wasn't there to observe him. He really wanted to play boules and asked lots of questions about the rules of the game.

He was very surprised to note that the dentist, whom everyone familiarly called Léon, was a player of the first order. From twenty metres, after three bouncing steps, he hit one of his adversary's boules after another, sending it rolling into the distance, and every time he then assumed a modest little expression, as if he considered the exploit perfectly natural.

The inspector went and drank a glass of white wine and found Charlot busy operating the fruit machine, while his companion, on the banquette, immersed herself in a film magazine. Had they been 'playing'?

'Isn't your friend with you?' said Paul, surprised.

For Mr Pyke too, it must have been like a holiday. He was with a fellow Englishman. He could speak his language and use expressions that had flavour only to two men who had attended the same college.

It was easy to predict the arrival of the *Cormoran*. The same phenomenon happened every time. They saw people passing, all making for the harbour. Then, once the boat was at the quay, the backward surge occurred. The same people passed in the reverse direction, this time with the newly disembarked passengers, carrying suitcases or parcels.

He followed the downward flow, not far from the mayor, pushing his inevitable handcart. He saw straight away, on the deck of the boat, Ginette and the inspector, who looked like a pair of friends. There were also some fishermen coming back from the funeral and two old spinsters, tourists for the Grand Hôtel.

In the group of those watching the disembarkation, he recognized Charlot, who had followed him and who, like him, seemed to be performing a ritual without really believing in it.

'Anything new, chief?' asked Lechat as soon as he landed. 'If you had any idea how hot it is over there!'

'Did it go well?'

Ginette stayed with them, quite naturally. She looked tired. A certain concern was apparent in her face.

All three of them made their way towards the Arche, and Maigret felt as if he had been taking this route daily for a very long time.

'Are you thirsty, Ginette?'

'I'd love a little aperitif.'

They drank it together, on the terrace, and Ginette was embarrassed because she kept feeling Maigret's eyes weighing down on her. He was looking at her with a dreamy, heavy gaze, like someone whose thoughts are far away.

'I'm going upstairs to freshen up,' she announced, once her glass was empty.

'Will you let me come with you?'

Lechat, who sensed something new in the air, tried to guess. He didn't dare question his boss. He stayed alone at the table, while Maigret, behind Ginette, climbed the stairs.

'You know,' she said once she was in the room, 'I really want to change.'

'That doesn't bother me.'

She pretended she was joking.

'What if it bothers me?'

Still, she took off her hat, then her dress, which he helped her to unhook at the back.

'It did affect me, though,' she sighed. 'I think he was happy here.'

On other evenings Marcellin, at this time of day, would have been taking part in the game of boules, in the square at sunset.

'Everyone was very kind. They liked him.'

She hurried to divest herself of her corset, which had left deep traces on her milky skin. Maigret turned his back towards her and faced the skylight.

'You remember the question I asked you?' he said in a neutral voice.

'You repeated it enough times. I wouldn't have believed that you could be so harsh.'

'For my part, I wouldn't have believed that you would try to hide something from me.'

'Did I hide something from you?'

'I asked you why you had come here, to Porquerolles, when Marcel's body was in Hyères.'

'I answered you.'

'You lied.'

'I don't know what you mean.'

'Why didn't you tell me about the phone call?'

'What phone call?'

'The one from Marcellin on the day of his death.'

'I forgot.'

'And the telegram too?'

He didn't need to turn round to know what her reaction was and he kept his eye fixed on the game of boules that was playing out in front of the terrace, from where a murmur of voices rose. There was the sound of clinking glasses.

It was very gentle, very reassuring, and Mr Pyke wasn't there. As the silence continued behind him, he asked:

'What are you thinking about?'

'I'm thinking that I was wrong, you know that.'

'Are you dressed?'

'Once I've put on my dress.'

He went and opened the door, to check that there was no one in the corridor. When he came back towards the middle of the room, Ginette was busy doing her hair at the mirror.

'You didn't talk about the Larousse?'

'To whom?'

'I don't know. Monsieur Émile, for example. Or Charlot.'

'I wasn't stupid enough to talk about it.'

'Because you hoped to replace Marcel? You do know, Ginette, that you're very self-interested?'

'That's what they always say about women when they try to ensure their future. And then jump on them when poverty makes them do a job that they haven't chosen.'

There was sudden bitterness in her voice.

'I thought you were going to marry Monsieur Émile?'

'On condition that Justine decided to die, and that at the last minute she didn't make arrangements to prevent her son from getting married. If you thought I did that out of the joy of my heart!'

'In short, if Marcel's tip was good and you were successful, you wouldn't get married?'

'Certainly not to that ugly brute.'

'Would you leave the house in Nice?'

'Without hesitation, I swear.'

'What would you do?'

'I'd go and live in the countryside, anywhere. I'd raise chickens and rabbits.'

'What did Marcellin say to you on the phone?'

'You'll claim that I'm lying again.'

He stared at her for a long time and then said:

'Not any more.'

'About time. He told me he had happened to discover an amazing thing. Those are the words he used. He added that it could bring in a lot of money, but that he hadn't yet decided.'

'Did he allude to anyone?'

'No. I never knew him to be so mysterious. He needed information. He asked me if we had a big Larousse, the one that's in I don't know how many volumes, at the house. I told him we didn't keep such a thing. Then he insisted that I go to the public library to consult it.'

'What did he want to know?'

'Too bad, isn't it? You've come so far that I don't stand a chance.'

'Not one, you're right.'

'Not counting the fact that I didn't understand a thing. I thought an idea would come to me once I was here.'

'Who died in 1890?'

'Did they show you my telegram? He didn't destroy it?'

'The post office kept a duplicate, as usual.'

'A certain Van Gogh, a painter. I read that he'd committed suicide. He was very poor, and today people fight over his canvases, which are worth I don't know how much. I wondered if Marcel had unearthed one.'

'And it wasn't the case?'

'I don't think so. When he phoned me he didn't even know that the gentleman was dead.'

'What did you think?'

'I don't know, I swear. Except I said to myself that if Marcel could make some money with that information I might be able to as well. Particularly when I found out that he'd been killed. He had no enemies. He had nothing to steal. You understand?'

'Do you imagine that the crime had something to do with the Van Gogh in question?'

Maigret wasn't being ironic. He took little puffs on his pipe, looking outside.

'You are probably right.'

'Too late, because you're here and it's no use to me any more. Do you still want me to stay on the island? Bear in mind that for me it's a holiday, and as long as you keep me here, the old vixen can't say a word to me.'

'In that case, stay.'

'Thank you. You're almost turning back into the person I knew in Paris.'

He didn't bother to return the compliment.

'Have a rest.'

He went down the stairs, passing close by Charlot, who looked at him mockingly, and went and sat down next to Lechat, on the terrace.

It was the most pleasurable time of day. The whole island was relaxed, and the sea around it, and the trees, the rocks, the ground of the square all seemed to breathe at a different rhythm after the heat of the day.

'Have you found out something new, chief?'

First of all Maigret ordered a drink from Jojo, who was passing close to him and looked as if she was angry with him for locking himself in the room with Ginette.

'I'm afraid so,' he sighed at last.

And as the inspector was looking at him in surprise:

'I mean that I probably won't be staying here for much longer. It's nice here, isn't it? On the other hand, there is Mr Pyke.'

It might be a good idea, because of Mr Pyke and what he would tell Scotland Yard, to bring the investigation to a prompt conclusion.

'There's a call for you from Paris, Monsieur Maigret.'

It was probably the information from Ostend.

8. Mr Pyke and the Grandmother

There was such a Sunday atmosphere that it was almost nauseating. Maigret liked to claim, half serious, half joking, that he had always had the ability to sniff out Sundays from the depths of his bed, without even having to open his eyes.

Here, something unexpected was happening with the bells. And yet they weren't real church bells, but feeble, tinkling bells like the ones in chapels or convents. It must have been because the quality, the density of the air wasn't the same as elsewhere. The hammer could be heard quite clearly striking the bronze, which gave out a random little note, but then the strange phenomenon began: a first ring appeared in the sky, which was pale and still cool, and stretched, hesitantly like a smoke-ring, became a perfect circle from which other circles emerged by magic, bigger and bigger, increasingly pure. The circles spread beyond the square and the houses, extended above the harbour and far out to sea, where little boats bobbed. They could be heard above the hills and the rocks, and they hadn't dispersed before the hammer struck the metal again and other circles of sound were born to recreate themselves, then still others that you listened to with innocent surprise, as you might have watched a firework display.

There was something paschal even in the simple sound

of footsteps on the uneven ground of the square, and Maigret, glancing at the window, expected to see first communicants getting their little legs caught up in their veils.

As he had done the previous day, he pulled on his slippers and trousers, put his waistcoat over his nightshirt with its red embroidered collar and went downstairs. As he entered the kitchen, he was disappointed. Unconsciously, he had wanted to start the previous morning all over again, find himself near the stove with Jojo making coffee, with the bright rectangle of the door opening on to the outside world. And yet here, today, there were five or six fishermen. They must have been served a glass of spirits, which gave a pungent scent to the atmosphere. On the tiles someone had knocked over a basket of fish: pink gurnards, some blue and green fish whose name Maigret didn't know, a kind of sea snake with red and yellow spots, which was still alive and rolling itself around the foot of a chair.

'Would you like a cup of coffee, Monsieur Maigret?'

It wasn't Jojo who was serving him, but the landlord. Perhaps because it was Sunday. Maigret felt like a thwarted child.

It happened to him sometimes, particularly in the morning, particularly when he approached the mirror to shave. He looked at his broad face, his big eyes, frequently with bags under them, his increasingly sparse hair. He was becoming severe, deliberately, as if to frighten himself. He said to himself: 'There you have the divisional detective chief inspector!'

Who would have dared not to take him seriously? Lots

of people, ones without easy consciences, trembled at the utterance of his name. He had the power to question them until they squealed with anxiety, to put them in prison, to send them to the guillotine.

On the island itself, there was now someone who heard as he did the sound of the bells, who inhaled the Sunday air, someone who was drinking the previous evening in the same room as him and who, in a few days, would be locked up behind bars once and for all.

He drank down his coffee, poured another, which he took to his room, and struggled to imagine that all of this was serious; not so long ago he had worn short trousers and crossed the square of his village, on chilly mornings, his fingertips frozen stiff, to go and serve mass in the little square that was lit entirely by candles.

Now, he was a grown-up, everyone believed him, and he, from time to time, was the only one hard to convince.

Did other people have the same impression? Did Mr Pyke, for example, sometimes wonder how he could be taken seriously? Did he, even rarely, have a sense that it was all just a game, 'life as a piece of fun'?

Was the major any different from one of those big children that you get in every class, one of those obese and sleepy boys that the teacher can't help but mock?

Mr Pyke had uttered a terrible phrase, the previous evening, just before the incident with Polyte. It was down below, when almost everyone had met up at the Arche as they had the evening before, as they did almost every evening. Of course, the inspector from Scotland Yard was sitting at the major's table, and at that moment, in spite of their difference in age and waist size, they looked as if they were related.

They must have been drinking, late in the afternoon, when Mr Pyke had gone to see his compatriot at his villa. Enough to have their vision blurred and their tongues thickened, but not enough to lose their dignity. At college they hadn't only been taught the same subjects, but later, God knows where, they had learned how to hold their alcohol in an identical manner.

They weren't maudlin; rather, they were wallowing in nostalgia, their thoughts miles away. They gave the impression of two deities who looked upon the agitation of the world with melancholy condescension. When Maigret came and sat down next to him, Mr Pyke had sighed, 'She's been a grandmother since last week.'

He avoided looking at the woman he was talking about, and whose name he avoided mentioning, but it could only have been Mrs Wilcox. She was there, on the other side of the room, sitting on the banquette beside Philippe. The Dutchman and Anna were sitting at the next table.

Mr Pyke had let a certain amount of time pass and had then added in the same neutral voice:

'Her daughter and son-in-law won't let her set foot in England. The major knows them very well.'

Poor old thing! Because suddenly they were discovering that Mrs Wilcox was in reality an old woman. They stopped making fun of her make-up, her dyed hair – with white roots showing – and her artificial excitement.

She was a grandmother, and Maigret remembered seeing his own in his mind's eye; he had tried to imagine his reaction as a child if someone had pointed to a woman like Mrs Wilcox and said, 'Go and kiss your grandma.'

She was forbidden to live in her own country and she didn't protest. She knew she wouldn't have the last word, that she was in the wrong. Like drunkards who are given just the necessary amount of pocket money and who try to cheat by asking for a little glass in this place and that.

Did she sometimes, as drunkards also do, feel sorry for her fate, weeping alone in her corner?

Perhaps when she had drunk a lot? Because she drank too. Philippe, if necessary, took on the task of filling her glass, while Anna, on the same banquette, thought only of one thing: the moment when she would go to bed at last.

Maigret was shaving. He hadn't had access to the only bathroom, which was occupied by Ginette.

'Five minutes!' she had called to him through the door.

From time to time he glanced down at the square, which was not the same colour as it had been on other days, even now that the bells had fallen silent. The priest was busy saying first mass. The priest in his own village got through it so quickly that young Maigret barely had time to give the response as he ran with the cruets.

A funny job he had! He was just a man like any other, and yet he held the fate of other men in his hands.

He had looked at them one by one, the previous evening. He hadn't drunk much, just enough to amplify his feelings a little. De Greef, with his sharply drawn profile, sometimes stared at him with faint irony and seemed to be challenging him. Philippe, in spite of his fine name and his ancestors, was a vulgar sort and he tried to make the best of it every time Mrs Wilcox ordered him around like a servant.

He must have taken his revenge at other times, of course, but he was no less obliged to swallow affronts in public.

What he had to swallow was considerable, so much so that everyone was embarrassed on his behalf. Poor Paul, who fortunately didn't have the first idea of what was going on, afterwards took all the trouble in the world to revive everyone's spirits.

They must have been talking about it, downstairs. The whole island would be talking about it all day. Would Polyte keep the secret? Now it didn't matter much. Polyte was at the bar, his captain's cap on his head, and he had already drained a few glasses; he was talking so loudly that his voice dominated all the conversations. On Mrs Wilcox's orders, Philippe had crossed the café to turn on the record player, as he was often required to do.

Then, after glancing at Maigret, Polyte had gone over to the record player and stopped him.

Then he had turned towards Moricourt and looked him sarcastically in the eye.

Philippe, without protesting, had pretended not to notice.

'I don't like people looking at me like that!' Polyte had said, stepping forwards a few steps.

'But . . . I'm not even looking at you . . .'

'You don't think I'm worth looking at?'

'I didn't say that.'

'You think I don't understand?'

Mrs Wilcox had murmured something in English to her companion. Mr Pyke had frowned.

'I suppose I'm not good enough for you, you little pimp?'

Very red in the face, Philippe didn't move, trying to look elsewhere.

'Are you trying to tell me again that I'm not good enough for you?'

At the same moment, de Greef had turned his head towards Maigret, in a particularly pointed manner. Had he understood? Lechat, who hadn't understood anything at all, had wanted to get up and intervene, and Maigret had had to grab his wrist under the table.

'What would you say if I smashed in that lovely face of yours, eh? What would you say to that?'

Then Polyte, who considered that the preliminaries had been satisfactorily attended to, brought his fist flying across the table into Philippe's face.

Philippe brought his hand to his nose. But that was all. He didn't try to defend himself, or to attack in turn. He stammered:

'I haven't done anything to you.'

Mrs Wilcox screamed, turning towards the bar:

'Monsieur Paul! Monsieur Paul! Will you throw out this maniac? It's an outrage.'

Her accent gave a special flavour to the words 'maniac' and 'outrage'.

'As to you . . .' Polyte began, turning towards the Dutchman.

The reaction was different. Without leaving his seat, de Greef hardened and said, 'All right, Polyte!'

It was clear that he wasn't going to put up with this and was ready to jump to his feet with all his muscles tensed.

Paul had intervened at last.

'Calm down, Polyte. Come to the kitchen for a moment. I need to talk to you.'

The captain went along, protesting for form's sake.

Lechat, who hadn't yet understood, had still asked thoughtfully:

'Is that your doing, chief?'

Maigret hadn't replied. He had assumed as benign an appearance as possible when the inspector from Scotland Yard had looked him in the eye.

Paul had made his apologies, as you must. They hadn't seen Polyte again; they must have ushered him out the back door. Today he would be presenting himself as a hero.

The fact remained that Philippe hadn't defended himself, that his face had sweated with fear for a moment, a physical fear that grips you in the hollow of your stomach and which you can't overcome.

After that he had drunk to excess, grim-faced, and in the end Mrs Wilcox had taken him home.

Nothing else had happened. Charlot and his dancer had gone to bed quite early, and when Maigret had gone up in turn they hadn't yet gone to sleep. Ginette and Monsieur Émile had been chatting in an undertone. No one had offered to buy a general round, perhaps because of the incident.

'Come in, Lechat,' Maigret shouted through the door.

Lechat had got himself ready.

'Has Mr Pyke gone for a swim?'

'He's downstairs, eating his bacon and eggs. I went to see off the *Cormoran*.'

'Nothing to note?

'Nothing. It seems that on Sunday lots of people come from Hyères and Toulon, people who dash to the beaches and litter them with sardine tins and empty bottles. You'll see them disembarking in an hour.'

The information from Ostende didn't contain anything unexpected. Monsieur Bebelmans, Anna's father, was an important person, who had been mayor of the town for a long time and who had once stood as a member of parliament. After his daughter left, he forbade the mention of her name in front of him. His wife was dead, and Anna hadn't been told.

'It seems that everyone who has gone off the rails for one reason or another ends up here,' observed Maigret, putting on his waistcoat.

'It's because of the climate!' replied Lechat, who was untroubled by such questions. 'I've been to see another revolver this morning.'

He was conscientious about his job. He took pains to find all the owners of revolvers. He went to see them one after the other and examined the guns, without too much hope, just because it is part of the routine.

'What are we doing today?'

Maigret, who was making for the door, avoided answering, and they found Mr Pyke sitting by the red checked tablecloth.

'I assume you're Protestant?' he said to him. 'In which case you won't be coming to high mass?'

'I am Protestant, and I went to low mass.'

Perhaps, if there had only been a synagogue, he would have gone there anyway, to attend a service, whatever it was, because it was Sunday.

'I don't know if you're going to want to come with me. This morning I have to pay a visit to a lady that you don't like meeting very much.'

'Are you going aboard the yacht?'

Maigret nodded, and Mr Pyke pushed away his plate, got to his feet and picked up the straw hat that he had bought the previous day in the mayor's shop, because he had already caught the sun so badly that his face was almost as red as the major's.

'Will you come with me?'

'Might you need a translator?'

'Can I come too?' asked Lechat.

'I'd rather you did, yes. Are you a good rower?'

'I was born by the sea.'

They walked to the harbour once again. It was Inspector Lechat who asked a fisherman's permission to use a boat without an engine, and the three men sat down in it. They could see de Greef and Anna having breakfast on the deck of their little boat.

The sea too, as if in honour of Sunday, had dressed in moiré satin; with each stroke of the oar, pearls sparkled in the sun. The *Cormoran* was on the other side of the water, by the Giens headland, waiting for the passengers who would get off the bus. They saw the bottom of the sea, the purple sea urchins in the hollows of the rocks, and sometimes a brilliant sea bass darting by. The bells rang to announce high mass, and all the houses must have smelled, with the morning coffee, of the perfume that the women put on their beautiful dresses.

The *North Star* looked much bigger, much taller when you pulled up alongside it, and since no one moved Lechat called out, raising his head:

'Hello!'

After a few moments a sailor leaned over the railing, one cheek covered with foam, and an open razor in his hand.

'Can we see your employer?'

'Couldn't you come back in an hour or two?'

Mr Pyke was visibly embarrassed. Maigret hesitated briefly, thinking about the 'grandmother'.

'We'll wait on deck if we have to,' he said to the sailor. 'Up you go, Lechat.'

They climbed the ladder one behind the other. There were portholes framed in copper in the deckhouse, and Maigret spotted a woman's face pressed against one of them for a moment, before disappearing into the darkness.

A moment later, the hatch opened, and Philippe's head appeared, his hair unkempt, his eyes still swollen with sleep.

'What do you want?' he asked sulkily.

'To speak to Mrs Wilcox.'

'She's not up yet.'

'That's not true. I've just seen her.'

Philippe was wearing silk pyjamas with blue stripes. There were a few steps to walk down to get into the cabin, and Maigret, heavy and stubborn, didn't wait to be invited.

'Will you allow me?'

It was a curious mixture of luxury and chaos, of refinement and squalor. The deck had been painstakingly scrubbed, and all the brasses gleamed, the rigging was neatly coiled, the command post with its compass and navigational instruments was as polished as a Dutch kitchen.

As soon as you went down the steps, you found yourself in a cabin with mahogany bulkheads, a table fixed to the ground and two banquettes upholstered with red leather, but there were bottles and glasses lying about on the table, there were slices of bread, an open tin of sardines, some playing cards; there was a disgusting smell, alcohol mixed with a whiff of bedroom.

They must have hurried to close the door of the neighbouring cabin, which served as a bedroom, and in running away Mrs Wilcox had left a satin slipper on the floor.

'Forgive me for disturbing you,' Maigret said politely to Philippe. 'You're probably having your breakfast?'

He looked without irony at the half-empty bottles of English beer, a slice of bread from which someone had taken a bite, a piece of butter wrapped in paper.

'Is this a search?' the young man asked, running his hand through his hair.

'It will be whatever you want it to be. So far, in my mind, it's just a visit.'

'At this time of day?'

'At this time of day some people are already tired!'

'Mrs Wilcox usually gets up late.'

They heard the sound of water on the other side of the door. Philippe would have liked to go and put on something more decent, but it would have meant revealing the excessively intimate chaos of the second cabin. He couldn't lay his hand on a dressing gown. His pyjamas were crumpled. He mechanically took a swig of beer. Lechat was still on deck, following Maigret's instructions, and he must have been questioning the two sailors.

They weren't English, as might have been assumed, but from Nice, probably of Italian origin, to judge by their accents.

'You may sit down, Mr Pyke,' said Maigret, as Philippe had forgotten to invite them to do so.

Maigret's grandmother always went to first mass, at six in the morning, and when you got up there she was in a black silk dress, with a white bonnet on her head, the fire blazing in the hearth, and lunch was served on a starched tablecloth.

Some old ladies here had been to first mass, and others were now crossing the square towards the open door of the church, from which the smell of incense emanated.

Mrs Wilcox had already drunk some beer, and in the morning the white roots of her dyed hair showed all the more. She moved about on the other side of the bulkhead, unable to be of any assistance to her secretary.

In striped pyjamas and with his cheek slightly swollen, where Polyte had punched him the previous evening, he looked like a sulky schoolboy. Because just as in all classes there is the fat boy who looks like a rubber ball, there is invariably the pupil who spends break-time skulking in a corner, while his schoolmates say, 'What a sneak!'

There were engravings hung on the bulkheads, but the

inspector was unable to judge their quality. Some were quite racy, but within the bounds of good taste.

They looked a little, he and Mr Pyke, as if they were in a waiting room, and the Englishman held his straw hat on his knees. At last Maigret lit his pipe.

'How old is your mother, Monsieur de Moricourt?'

'Why are you asking me that?'

'No reason. Judging by your age, she must be about fifty?'

'Forty-five. She had me very young. She got married at sixteen.'

'Mrs Wilcox is older, isn't she?'

Mr Pyke lowered his head. It was as if the inspector was doing it on purpose, to pile on the embarrassment. Lechat was more at ease, outside, sitting on the railing, chatting with one of the two sailors, who was cleaning his nails in the sun.

At last there was a sound against the door, and it opened. Mrs Wilcox appeared and closed it quickly behind her so that they wouldn't see the chaos.

She had had time to get dressed, to wash, but her features, under the thick make-up, were still puffy, her eyes anxious.

She must have been pitiful in the morning, when she treated her hangover with a bottle of strong beer.

'Grandmother . . .' Maigret thought in spite of himself.

He got to his feet, greeted her and introduced his companion.

'I don't suppose you've met Mr Pyke? He's a compatriot of yours, he's at Scotland Yard. He isn't here in an official capacity. Sorry to disturb you so early, Mrs Wilcox.'

She remained, in spite of everything, a woman of the

world, and a glance was enough to let Philippe know that his outfit was unsatisfactory.

'Will you let me go and get dressed?' he murmured, with a surly glance at the inspector.

'You might feel more at ease.'

'Sit down, gentlemen. Can I offer you something?'

She noticed the pipe which Maigret was allowing to go out.

'Go on smoking, please. I'm about to light a cigarette anyway.'

She managed to smile.

'Please forgive all this chaos, but a yacht isn't a house, and space is limited.'

What was Mr Pyke thinking at that precise moment? That his French colleague was a brute, or a boor?

It was very possible. In any case Maigret wasn't all that proud of the work he had to do.

'I think you know Jef de Greef, Mrs Wilcox?'

'He's an accomplished fellow, and Anna is nice. They've been on board a few times.'

'They say he's a talented painter.'

'I believe so. I had the chance to buy a painting from him, and I would happily have shown it to you if I hadn't sent it to my villa in Fiesole.'

'You have a villa in Italy?'

'Oh! It's a very modest villa. But it is magnificently situated, on the hill, and from the windows you can see the whole panorama of Florence. Do you know Florence, inspector?'

'I haven't had the pleasure.'

'I live there for part of the year. It's where I send everything I manage to buy in the course of my wanderings.'

She thought she had found solid ground.

'You really wouldn't like a drink?'

She herself was thirsty and was eyeing up the beer that she hadn't had time to finish just now and didn't dare to drink alone.

'Wouldn't you like to try the beer that I have imported directly from England?'

He said he would, to please her. She went to fetch some bottles from a cupboard converted into an ice box. Most of the bulkheads in the cabin were really wardrobes, just as the banquettes concealed chests.

'You buy a lot of things when you're travelling, don't you?'

She laughed.

'Who told you that? I buy for the pleasure of buying, that's true. In Istanbul, for example, I always allow myself to be tempted by the merchants in the bazaar. I come back on board with some horrors. In situ they look lovely. Then, when I reach the villa and find these things . . .'

'Did you meet Jef de Greef in Paris?'

'No. Just here, not long ago.'

'And your secretary?'

'He's been with me for two years. He's a very cultured boy. We met in Cannes.'

'Was he working?'

'He was writing an article for a Paris newspaper.'

Moricourt must have had his ear pressed to the bulkhead.

'You have a perfect command of French, Mrs Wilcox.'

'I did part of my studies in Paris. My governess was French.'

'Did Marcellin often come on board?'

'Certainly. I think almost everyone on the island has been on board.'

'Do you remember the night when he died?'

'I think so.'

He looked at her hands, which weren't trembling.

'He talked a lot about me that evening.'

'That's what I was told. I didn't know who you were. I asked Philippe.'

'And Monsieur de Moricourt knew?'

'Apparently you're famous.'

'When you left the Arche de Noé . . .'

'I'm listening.'

'Had Marcellin left already?'

'I couldn't say. What I do know is that we were pressing ourselves against the houses when we came down to the harbour, the mistral was so strong. I was even worried that we wouldn't be able to get back on board.'

'You embarked straight away, you and Monsieur de Moricourt?'

'Straight away. What else would we have done? It reminds me that Marcellin came with us to the dinghy.'

'You didn't meet anyone?'

'There couldn't have been anyone outside in that weather.'

'De Greef and Anna were back on their boat?'

'It's possible. I don't remember. Wait . . .'

Then Maigret was startled to hear the precise voice of Mr Pyke, who was allowing himself to take part in his investigation for the first time. The man from the Yard said calmly, but without seeming to attach any importance to it:

'Back home, Mrs Wilcox, we would be obliged to remind you that anything you say could be used against you.'

She looked at him, stunned, then looked at Maigret, and there was something like madness in her eyes.

'Am I being questioned?' she asked. 'But tell me, inspector . . . I assume you don't suspect us, Philippe and me, of killing a man?'

Maigret was silent for a moment and examined his pipe carefully.

'I don't suspect someone without a reason, Mrs Wilcox. But yes, you are being questioned, and you have the right not to reply.'

'Why would I not reply? We came back straight away. Even though the dinghy had taken water when we climbed in, and we had to cling to the ladder to get on board.'

'Philippe didn't leave again?'

There was hesitation in her eyes. She was embarrassed by the presence of her compatriot.

'We went to bed straight away, and he couldn't have left the boat without me hearing him.'

Philippe chose that moment to appear, in white flannel trousers, with his hair slicked back and a cigarette that he had just lit between his lips. He wanted to appear respectable. He addressed Maigret directly.

'Do you have questions to ask me, inspector?'

Maigret pretended to ignore him.

'Do you often buy paintings?'

'Quite often. It's a foible of mine. Even if I don't have what you would call a gallery of paintings, I have some quite good ones.'

'In Fiesole?'

'In Fiesole, yes.'

'Italian masters?'

'I don't go that far. I'm more modest; I stick to quite modern pictures.'

'Cézannes or Renoirs, for example?'

'I have a delightful little Renoir.'

'Degas, Manet, Monet?'

'A Degas drawing, a dancer.'

'Van Gogh?'

Maigret wasn't looking at her but staring at Philippe, who seemed to be swallowing his saliva, his gaze completely frozen.

'I've just bought a Van Gogh.'

'How long ago?'

'A few days. Which day did we go to Hyères to send it, Philippe?'

'I don't remember exactly,' he replied in a toneless voice.

Maigret helped them.

'Wasn't it one or two days before Marcellin's death?'

'Two days before,' she said. 'I remember.'

'Did you find the painting here?'

She had no time to reflect and a moment later she bit her lip.

'It was Philippe,' she began. 'Through a friend, he . . .'

She understood, from the silence of the three men, looked at each them in turn and cried out:

'What is it, Philippe?'

She had sprung to her feet and walked towards the inspector.

'You don't mean . . .? Explain yourself! Speak! Why aren't you saying anything? Philippe! What . . .?'

Philippe still hadn't moved.

'I'm sorry for taking your secretary away, madame.'

'You're arresting him? Because I tell you, he was here, he didn't leave me all night.'

She looked at the door of the cabin that served as a bedroom and she seemed to be about to open it, to show the big bed, to cry out:

'How could he have left without my knowing?'

Maigret and Mr Pyke had risen to their feet as well.

'Will you follow me, Monsieur de Moricourt?'

'Do you have a warrant?'

'I will ask the magistrate for one if you insist, but I don't think you will.'

'Are you arresting me?'

'Not yet.'

'Where are you taking me?'

'Somewhere where we can talk calmly. You don't think that's preferable?'

'Tell me, Philippe . . .' began Mrs Wilcox.

She began to talk to him in English, without realizing. Philippe wasn't listening, wasn't looking at her, was no longer concerned with her. As he climbed on deck he didn't look back.

'It won't help you much,' he said to Maigret.

'That's quite possible.'

'Are you going to handcuff me?'

It was still Sunday, and the *Cormoran*, moored at the jetty, was disgorging its passengers in their lightly coloured clothes. Tourists, perched on the rocks, were already fishing.

Mr Pyke was last to leave the cabin and when he took his seat in the dinghy he was very red in the face. Lechat, surprised to have one extra passenger, didn't know what to say.

Maigret, sitting at the back, dipped his left hand in the water, as he did when he was little and his father took him out in a boat on the pond.

The bells were still circling in the sky.

9. Maigret's Bad Pupils

They stopped outside the grocer's shop to ask the mayor for the key. He was serving customers and called something to his wife, who was little and pale, with her hair in a tight bun at the back of her neck. She looked for a long time. Meanwhile Philippe stood waiting, between Maigret and Mr Pyke, wearing a stubborn expression and a sulky air, and it looked more than ever like a scene at school, with the punished pupil and the heavy, implacable headmaster.

You would never have thought that so many people could come off the *Cormoran*. It is true that other boats had made the crossing that morning. Until the tourists had time to channel themselves off towards the beaches, the square looked like the scene of an invasion.

They spotted Anna, in the gloom of the Cooperative, with her shopping net, wearing her pareo, while de Greef was sitting with Charlot on the terrace of the Arche.

Those two had seen Philippe passing by between the policemen. They had watched after him. They were free, with a bottle of chilled wine on the café table in front of them.

Maigret had muttered a few words to Lechat, who had stayed behind.

At last the mayor's wife brought the key, and, a few

moments later, Maigret pushed open the door of the town hall, immediately opening the window because of the smell of dust and mildew.

'Sit down, Moricourt.'

'Is that an order?'

'Very much so.'

He pushed towards him one of the folding chairs that were used at the 14th of July celebrations. It seemed that Mr Pyke had worked out that in these circumstances the inspector didn't like to see people standing up, for he in turn unfolded a chair and went and sat down in a corner.

'I don't suppose you have anything to tell me?'

'Am I under arrest?'

'Yes.'

'I didn't kill Marcellin.'

'Go on.'

'Nothing. I'm not saying anything more. You can question me as much as you like and use all the revolting means at your disposal to make people talk, but I'm saying nothing.'

Like a spoilt child! Perhaps because of what he had seen that morning, Maigret couldn't take him seriously, he couldn't get his head around the fact that he was dealing with a grown man.

The inspector didn't sit down. He walked aimlessly back and forth, touching a rolled-up flag or the bust of Marianne. He stopped for a moment at the window and saw little girls dressed in white crossing the square under the watchful eye of two nuns in cornettes. He hadn't been entirely wrong just now when he had thought about first communion.

The people of the island, that morning, were wearing clean canvas trousers of a blue that became deep and sumptuous in the sun of the square, and the white shirts were dazzling. They were already starting to play boules. Monsieur Émile was making his slow way towards the post office.

'I suppose you realize that you're a scoundrel?'

Maigret, enormous, standing right next to Philippe, looked him from top to bottom, and the young man instinctively raised his hands to protect his face.

'I really mean a scoundrel, a frightened, cowardly scoundrel. There are people who burgle flats, and they at least take a risk. Others focus on old ladies, steal rare books from them with a view to selling them on and, when they are caught, start crying, pleading for forgiveness and to be allowed to talk to their poor mothers.'

Mr Pyke seemed to be making himself as small, as still as possible so as not to get in his colleague's way. His breathing wasn't even audible, but the sounds of the island came in through the open window and mingled strangely with the inspector's voice.

'Who came up with the idea of the fake paintings?'

'I'll only talk in the presence of a lawyer.'

'So that your unfortunate mother will have to bleed herself dry to pay for a famous lawyer! Because nothing but a famous lawyer would do, is that right? You're a repellent character, Moricourt!'

He walked with his hands behind his back, more of a headmaster than ever.

'At school we had a classmate who was like you. Like

you, he was a sneak. Now and again he needed correction, and when we gave it to him our teacher was careful to turn his back or leave the playground. You got one yesterday evening and you didn't move. You stood there, pale and trembling, on the spot, beside that old woman who keeps you alive. I was the one who asked Polyte to give you a slap, because I needed to see your reaction, because I wasn't yet sure.'

'Are you planning on hitting me again?'

It was bravado, but he was clearly terrified.

'There are various kinds of scoundrel, Moricourt, and unfortunately some of them we never manage to send to jail. I can tell you straight away that I will do everything in my power to make sure that's where you end up.'

Ten times he came back towards the seated young man, who each time made an instinctive gesture to protect his face.

'Admit that the idea of the paintings came from you.'

'I find your tone overly familiar.'

'You'll have to admit it in the end, if it takes three days and three nights. I've met one like you before, only tougher. He showed off too when he came to Quai des Orfèvres. He was well dressed, like you. It took a long time. There were five or six of us in relay. After thirty-six hours, do you know what happened to him? Do you know how we found out that he was losing his nerve? By the smell! A smell as revolting as he was! He had just soiled his trousers.'

He looked at Moricourt's fine white trousers and ordered him point-blank:

'Take off your tie.'

'Why?'

'Do you want me to do it for you? Fine! Now, unlace your shoes. Pull the laces out. You'll see that in a few hours you'll start looking guilty.'

'You have no right . . .'

'I'm giving myself the right! You wondered how to pump more money out of the mad old woman you're hooked up with. Your lawyer will probably argue that it's immoral to leave fortunes in the hands of women like her and he'll claim that it's an irresistible temptation. That needn't concern us for the time being. That's for the jury. Because she bought paintings but had no expertise, you told yourself that there was big money to be made, and you made contact with de Greef. I wonder if it wasn't you who brought him to Porquerolles.'

'De Greef is a little saint, isn't he?'

'Another kind of scoundrel. How many forgeries has he made for your old mistress?'

'I told you I wasn't going to say.'

'The Van Gogh couldn't have been the first. Except that someone spotted that one, probably before it was quite finished. Marcellin hung about all over the place. He was as likely to climb aboard de Greef's yacht as he was to climb aboard the *North Star*. I assume he surprised the Dutchman signing a canvas with a name that wasn't his. Then he saw the same painting on Mrs Wilcox's boat, and that worried him. It took him a while to work out the fraud. He wasn't sure. He had never heard of Van Gogh and called a friend to find out.'

Philippe stared at the floor with a surly expression.

'I'm not claiming it was you who killed him.'

'I didn't kill him.'

'You're probably too cowardly to do such a thing. Marcellin said to himself that since you were both due to clean up on the back of the old woman there was no reason why there shouldn't be a third. He told you that. You wouldn't go along with it. So, just to dot the 'i's, he started talking about his friend Maigret. How much was Marcellin asking for?'

'No comment.'

'I have all the time in the world. Marcellin was killed that night.'

'I have an alibi.'

'In fact, at the time of his death, you were in the grandmother's bed.'

The smell of the aperitifs being served on the terrace of the Arche reached all the way to the little room in the town hall. De Greef must still have been there. Perhaps Anna had joined him with the shopping? Lechat, at a nearby table, had an eye on him and would stop him leaving if necessary.

As for Charlot, he would surely have understood by now that he had turned up too late. Someone else had had his eyes on his share!

'Are you planning on talking, Philippe!'

'No.'

'Bear in mind that I'm not trying to trick you into making a confession. I'm not telling you that we have proof, that de Greef gave you away. You'll end up talking because you're a coward, because you're poisonous. Give me your cigarettes.'

Maigret took the pack that the young man handed to him and threw it out of the window.

'Can I ask you for a favour, Mr Pyke? Would you ask Lechat, who is sitting on the terrace of the Arche, to bring the Dutchman in? Without the young woman. I'd also like Jojo to bring us some bottles of beer.'

As if out of scruple, he didn't say a word during his colleague's absence. He went on pacing back and forth, hands behind his back, and Sunday life went on outside the window.

'Come in, de Greef. If you have a tie, I would ask you to take it off, as well as your boot laces.'

'Am I under arrest?'

Maigret merely nodded.

'Sit down. Not too near your friend Philippe. Give me your cigarettes and the one you have in your mouth.'

'Do you have a warrant?'

'I'm going to have one sent by telegram, in both your names, lest there be any more doubt on the matter.'

He sat down in the seat that the mayor must have occupied during weddings.

'One of you killed Marcellin. To tell the truth, it doesn't really matter who, because you're each as guilty as the other.'

Jojo came in with a tray covered with bottles and glasses and stood open-mouthed at the sight of the two young men.

'Don't be scared, Jojo. They're only dirty little murderers. Don't mention it outside straight away, so we don't have the whole population outside the window, and the Sunday tourists to boot.'

Maigret took his time and looked at the young men in turn. The Dutchman was much calmer and showed no sign of bravado.

'Maybe I should leave you to sort that one out between you? Because without question, it was one of you two. And one of you, in fact, will probably lose his head, or end up behind bars for the rest of his days, while the other will get away with a few years in prison. Which one?'

The sneak was already shifting on his chair, like a schoolboy about to put his hand up.

'Unfortunately the law doesn't take actual responsibility into account. For my part, I'd happily make you both carry the can, although with the difference that I would have a little bit of sympathy for de Greef.'

Philippe was still shifting, uneasy, visibly disconcerted.

'Admit it, de Greef, you didn't do it only for the money, did you? No reply either? As you wish. I bet you've been enjoying yourself producing fake paintings for ages, to prove to yourself that you aren't a Sunday painter, a worthless dauber. Have you sold many?

'It doesn't matter! What better revenge on the people who don't understand you than to see one of your paintings, signed by an illustrious name, hanging in the Louvre or a museum in Amsterdam!

'We'll see your latest works. We'll have them brought from Fiesole. Our experts will discuss them in court. You're going to have a lot of fun, de Greef!'

It was almost amusing to see Philippe's face, both disgusted and vexed, during this speech. Both looked like children more than ever. Philippe was jealous of the words that Maigret was addressing to his fellow pupil and must have been stifling his protests.

'Admit it, Monsieur de Greef, you're not altogether unhappy that all this is coming out, are you?'

Even that 'Monsieur' cut Moricourt to the depth of his being.

'When you're the only one who knows, it isn't much fun in the end. You don't love your life, Monsieur de Greef.'

'Nor yours, nor the one they would have liked me to have.'

'You don't love anything.'

'I don't love myself.'

'And you don't love that little girl that you only snatched from her family out of defiance, to infuriate her parents. For how long have you wanted to kill another person? I don't mean out of necessity, to earn money or get rid of an awkward witness. I'm talking about killing for killing's sake, to see how it works, what you feel while you're doing it. And even to hit the corpse with a hammer afterwards to prove that you have nerves of steel.'

The Dutchman's lips spread into a thin smile, and Philippe watched from the corner of his eye, uncomprehending.

'Now, do you want me to tell you both what's going to happen? You've both decided not to say anything. You're convinced that there is no proof against you. No one witnessed Marcellin's death. No one on the island heard the shot, because of the mistral. They haven't found the gun, which is probably safe at the bottom of the sea. I haven't taken the trouble to do a search. The fingerprints won't help either. Preparations for the trial will take a long time. The judge will patiently cross-question you, he will find out about your track record, and the newspapers will talk about you a lot. They won't neglect to stress that you are both of good family.

'Your friends in Montparnasse, de Greef, will emphasize the fact that you are gifted. You will be represented as an eccentric, misunderstood person. They will also talk about the two little volumes of verse that Moricourt published.'

You would have thought he would be happy to see a good point of his being stressed at last!

'The journalists will go and interview the judge at the court in Groningen, Madame de Moricout in Saumur. In the yellow press they will make fun of Mrs Wilcox, and doubtless her embassy will take measures to ensure that her name is mentioned as little as possible.'

He drank down half a glass of beer and went and sat down on the window-sill, with his back to the sunlit square.

'De Greef will remain silent, because it's his temperament, because he isn't afraid.'

'And I will talk?' sniggered Philippe.

'You will talk. Because you look like a sneak, because everyone will see you as the repellent character you are, because you will want to cut your losses, because you're a coward and because you will be convinced that by talking you will save your precious skin.'

De Greef turned towards his companion with an indefinable smile on his lips.

'You will probably start speaking tomorrow, when you

find yourself in a real police station, and a few stout fellows question you with their fists. You don't like fists, Philippe.'

'You have no right.'

'Neither do you have the right to swindle a poor woman who no longer knows what she's doing.'

'Or who knows only too well. It's because she has money that you're coming to her defence.'

Maigret didn't need to approach him for him to raise both his arms again.

'You will speak, especially when you see that de Greef has a better chance than you do of getting away with it.'

'He was on the island.'

'He had an alibi as well. If you were with the old woman, he was with Anna . . .'

'Anna will say . . .'

'Say what?'

'Nothing.'

Lunch had begun at the Arche. Either Jojo couldn't have kept her mouth shut completely, or else people sensed something, because every now and again shadowy outlines could be seen roaming around the town hall.

In a moment there would be a crowd.

'I would like to leave the two of you alone. What do you think, Mr Pyke? With someone to keep an eye on them, obviously, because otherwise we risk finding them in little pieces. Will you stay, Lechat?'

Lechat went and took his place, with both elbows on the table and, for want of an aperitif or a white wine, poured himself a glass of beer.

Outside, Maigret and his British colleague found the sun

at its warmest and strolled for a few moments without a word.

'Are you disappointed, Mr Pyke?' the inspector asked with a little sidelong glance.

'Why?'

'I don't know. You came to France to find out about our methods, and you will have observed that we don't have any. Moricourt will speak. I could have made him speak straight away.'

'Using the method you mentioned?'

'That one or some other. Whether he talks or not, it doesn't matter. He will retract his confession. He will confess again, and retract again. You will see that doubts will be planted in the jury's mind. The two lawyers will argue like cat and dog, each whitewashing his client, each placing all responsibility on his colleague's client.'

They didn't need to stand on tiptoe to see, through the town-hall window, the two young men sitting on their chairs. On the terrace of the Arche, Charlot was having his lunch, with his girlfriend on his right, and on his left Ginette, who seemed to be explaining to the inspector from a distance that she hadn't been able to refuse his invitation.

'It's nicer to deal with professionals.'

Perhaps it was Charlot that he had in mind.

'But they are rarely the ones who kill. True crimes come about more or less by chance. Those kids started by playing, without trying to guess where it would lead them. It all felt a bit like a great game. Passing off paintings signed by illustrious names on a mad old woman with millions to spend! And then one morning some random chap, a Marcellin, climbs on deck at an inopportune moment . . .'

'Do you feel sorry for them?'

Maigret shrugged, without replying.

'You will see that psychiatrists will talk about their respective levels of responsibility.'

Mr Pyke, who was squinting into the sun, stared at his colleague for a long time, as if trying to penetrate the depths of his thought, and then said simply: 'Ah!'

The inspector didn't ask him what conclusions he had drawn. He talked about something else and asked:

'Do you like the Mediterranean, Mr Pyke?'

And as Mr Pyke hesitantly sought his reply, he went on:

'I wonder if the climate isn't too strong for me. We'll certainly be able to leave this evening.'

The white bell-tower looked like a diamond set into the sky, which was made of a material that was both hard and transparent. The mayor, intrigued, looked from outside, through the window, into his town hall. What was Charlot doing? They saw him getting up from his table and walking swiftly towards the harbour.

Maigret looked at him for a moment, frowning, and murmured:

'As long as . . .'

He hurried in the same direction, followed by Mr Pyke, who didn't understand.

When they came within view of the jetty, Charlot was already on the deck of the little yacht amusingly christened *Fleur d'amour*.

He leaned over the railing for a moment, looked inside,

disappeared and came back on to the deck carrying someone in his arms.

When the two men arrived in their turn, Anna was lying on the deck, and Charlot shamelessly tore off her pareo, revealing, in the sunlight, a heavy, full bosom.

'You didn't think about that?' he said bitterly.

'Veronal?'

'There's an empty tube on the cabin floor.'

There were five, then ten, then a whole crowd around Mademoiselle Bebelmans. The island doctor came tripping along and said mournfully, 'I brought an emetic, just in case.'

Mrs Wilcox was on the deck of her yacht, with one of her sailors, and they were passing a pair of marine binoculars to one another.

'You see, Mr Pyke, I make mistakes as well? She had worked out that de Greef had nothing to fear but her testimony and she was too frightened to talk.'

He parted the crowd that had assembled in front of the town hall. Lechat had closed the window. The two young men were still in their seats, the bottles of beer on the table.

Maigret started pacing the room like a bear, stopped in front of Philippe de Moricourt and, suddenly, with no warning, before the man could protect himself, slapped him full in the face.

With that out of his system, in an almost calm voice, he murmured:

'I'm sorry, Mr Pyke.'

Then, to de Greef, who was watching him and trying to understand:

'Anna is dead.'

He decided not to question them that day. He tried not to see the coffin, which was still in its corner, old Benoît's famous coffin, which had already been used for Marcellin and which would now be used for the girl from Ostend.

As if by a twist of irony, the bearded face of Benoît, still very much alive, was recognizable in the crowd. Lechat and the two men, cuffs around their wrists, were making their way towards the Giens headland aboard a fishing boat.

Maigret and Mr Pyke took the *Cormoran* at five o'clock, and Ginette was on it, as well as Charlot and his dancer, and all the tourists who had spent the day on the beaches of the island.

The *North Star* bobbed at anchor by the entrance to the harbour. Maigret, frowning, smoked his pipe, and as his lips were moving Mr Pyke leaned towards him and asked:

'I'm sorry? Did you say something?'

'I said: the little brats!'

After which, very quickly, he turned his head and looked at the bottom of the water.

INSPECTOR MAIGRET

OTHER TITLES IN THE SERIES

A MAN'S HEAD
GEORGES SIMENON

He stared at Maigret, who stared back and found no trace of drunkenness in his companion's face.

Instead he saw the same eyes ablaze with acute intelligence which were now fixed on him with a look of consummate irony, as though Radek were truly possessed by fierce exultant joy.

An audacious plan to prove the innocence of a young drifter awaiting execution takes Maigret through the grey, autumnal streets of Paris. As he pursues the true culprit from lonely docks to elegant hotels and fashionable bars, he confronts the destructive power of a dangerously sharp intellect.

Translated by David Coward

INSPECTOR MAIGRET

OTHER TITLES IN THE SERIES

THE SHADOW PUPPET
GEORGES SIMENON

'One by one the lighted windows went dark. The silhouette of the dead man could still be seen through the frosted glass like a Chinese shadow puppet . . . A young woman crossed the courtyard with hurried steps, leaving a whiff of perfume in her wake.'

Summoned to the dimly-lit Place des Vosges one night, Maigret uncovers a tragic story of desperate lives, unhappy families, addiction and a terrible, fatal greed.

Translated by Ros Schwartz

INSPECTOR MAIGRET

OTHER TITLES IN THE SERIES

THE SAINT-FIACRE AFFAIR
GEORGES SIMENON

'Maigret savoured the sensations of his youth again: the cold stinging eyes, frozen fingertips, an aftertaste of coffee. Then, stepping inside the church, a blast of heat, soft light; the smell of candles and incense.'

The last time Maigret went home to the village of his birth was for his father's funeral. Now an anonymous note predicting a crime during All Souls' Day mass draws him back there, where troubling memories resurface and hidden vices are revealed.

Translated by Shaun Whiteside

OTHER TITLES IN THE SERIES

LIBERTY BAR
GEORGES SIMENON

'It smelled of holidays. The previous evening Cannes harbour, with the setting sun, had also had that smell of holidays, especially the Ardena, whose owner swaggered in front of two girls with gorgeous figures.'

Maigret is dazzled by the Côte d'Azur, but behind the perfect façade of sun-drenched villas, palm-lined promenades and luxury cars, he discovers the dark reality of a man who can't escape his past any more.

Translated by David Watson

OTHER TITLES IN THE SERIES

MAIGRET
GEORGES SIMENON

'It was indeed Maigret who was beside him, smoking his pipe, his velvet collar upturned, his hat perched on his head. But it wasn't an enthusiastic Maigret. It wasn't even a Maigret who was sure of himself.'

Maigret's peaceful retirement in the country is interrupted when his nephew comes to him for help after being implicated in a crime he didn't commit. Soon Maigret is back in the heart of Paris, and out of place in a once-familiar world...

Translated by Ros Schwartz

INSPECTOR MAIGRET

OTHER TITLES IN THE SERIES